THE MYSTERY ON APACHE CANYON DRIVE

A MYSTERY SEARCHERS BOOK

BARRY FORBES

ST LEO PRESS

A MYSTERY SEARCHERS BOOK

VOLUME 1

THE MYSTERY ON APACHE CANYON DRIVE

The Mystery on Apache Canyon Drive
© 2019 Barry Forbes

DISCLAIMER

Prescott, the former capital of the Arizona Territory, is considered by many to be the state's crown jewel. Aside from this Central Arizona locale, *The Mystery Searchers Book Series* is a work of fiction. Names, characters, businesses, places, events, incidents, and other locales are either the products of the author's imagination or used in a fictitious manner. Any resemblance to actual persons, living or dead, or actual events is purely coincidental.

———

Register for monthly drawings of free books, Amazon gift cards and other prizes plus email alerts at www.MysterySearchers.com

———

DEDICATION

For Linda,

Whose steadfast love and encouragement
made this series possible.

1

THE RESCUE

A rare heat wave had smothered the northern Arizona countryside, shimmering in giant waves off the roadway ahead. Billowing, bright white clouds raced overhead, tracking Highway 89 as it ran through scenic boulder country. Natural canyon murals rippled past along both sides of the winding route.

Suzanne was at the wheel, thankful the early afternoon traffic was lighter than normal. The twins cranked up the radio. They often took turns driving the car, a recent surprise for their sixteenth birthday. The present had appeared on that day when their father, Edward Jackson—*Chief* Edward Jackson of the Prescott City Police, that is—parked the gleaming white sedan in the driveway.

"Best used vehicle out there," he said with a wide grin. "It's a Chevy. Solid protection with low mileage."

Elated beyond belief, Suzanne's twin brother, Tom, couldn't wait to get behind the wheel.

"Thanks, Dad!" he exclaimed. "We'll take turns driving. I'm first."

"Good luck with that," Suzanne said with a laugh, beating her brother to the punch. She grabbed the keys from her father and jumped into the driver's seat, her auburn ponytail tossing behind her.

"What the heck, Suzie," Tom protested, employing a favorite nickname for his twin sister. "Why should you be first?"

"Because I was born first."

"Very funny."

"I thought so."

She was right, of course. The twins, born five minutes apart, had arrived in the world with masses of thick, dark hair that had lightened over the years. Now, Tom wore his short, while Suzanne's hair was long enough to be the envy of her girlfriends. They bore a startling resemblance to their mother but had inherited their father's height. "Good thing it wasn't the other way around!" the Chief had joked more than once.

At Prescott High, Suzanne worked hard to maintain her B average and excelled at tennis and track. She was the type of person who knew where she was going in life. When friends thought of the outgoing girl, one word came to mind: *confident*. "Just as long as your temper doesn't get in the way," her mother had often warned. Which it often did—as a small child, her parents called her "the spitfire." Things had improved with the passing of time. Still, every so often...

Tom was the quiet, thoughtful type. Growing up, he fought hard to overcome a natural shyness—easy to ignore because his sister was the polar opposite. But technology helped—a lot. For Tom, technology was... well, *intuitive*. Like a duck to water. He learned to code in grade school and became a founding member of Prescott High's prestigious high tech club in his freshman year—the same year they won a national robotics competition. "If there's a technical issue in the family, Tom's our guy," his sister often said. "And he understands remotes, which is huge."

Prescott, Arizona is one of those sleepy little cities where nothing much ever seems to happen. Unless, of course, your father happens to be the chief of police. Then it's a whole different ballgame.

As they grew up, somehow the drama of crime and law enforcement had slipped into the twins everyday life. At dinnertime, their questions would fly:

"Okay, tell us, Dad. Are they guilty?"

"How did you catch them?"

"What happened? How'd they pull it off?"

The Chief smiled at their curiosity. "Sorry, maybe someday."

With almost all the facts concealed from their knowledge, a case could swirl into an obscuring fog that kept the twins guessing for weeks on end. They both loved mysteries and shared an ambition: to follow their father's footsteps into law enforcement. Somehow, that day always seemed a long way in the future.

Today, at last, summer vacation had arrived. It was the first Monday in June, with their calendars chock-full and friends waiting. In fact, the technology club president, Ray Huntley, had scheduled the first summer meeting for that same morning. But Suzanne needed the car to meet her best friend, Kathy Brunelli.

"Seriously?" Tom said, surprise crossing his face. "How come you never mentioned it before?"

"Seriously," Suzanne replied. "And I told you yesterday, but your head was off in the Cloud. But not to worry, I'll drop you off."

"Oh, man," Tom groaned. Always on time no matter what, he glanced at the kitchen clock. The morning was slipping away. "Okay, but I can't be late."

His sister rattled the keys. "You bet. I'm ready, bro." That was her favorite nickname for her brother—except when they argued. Then she called him "hotshot."

Ray lived on a ranch a few miles north of the city, half an hour from the Jacksons'. It was a typical Arizona day, warm and pleasant, and the marbled walls of the narrow canyon they were now heading into were enough to take away anyone's breath.

"Just ten more minutes," said Suzanne. "I'll get you there on— *What is that?"* She sat bolt upright, her eyes riveted to the road ahead. A second earlier, the margins of the twisting highway had been empty. Something was rippling the tall, rangy grass in the ditch not far out front. Suzanne tapped her brake pedal. *A deer?* She gripped the steering wheel fiercely and caught her breath.

Tom's eyes were locked on his cell phone—he was busy messaging Pete Brunelli, Kathy's brother, and Tom's best friend— but his sister's tone rattled him. He tensed and looked up, staring hard through the windshield. "What? I don't see any—"

"*It's a child!*" Suzanne cried. A small head with short black hair had poked up from the tall grass.

Tom felt the car wobble and instinctively tensed. Without warning, the child sprang from the grass and swerved onto the blacktop, racing across the highway before them. Suzanne's mouth went dry, the hair rose on the back of her neck. She stomped on the brakes, hard, glancing from the windshield to her rearview mirror: *No traffic coming from either direction.* She flipped her four-way flashers on and angled toward the center lines, screeching to an abrupt stop.

The twins darted out of the car, leaving both doors flung wide open, and sprinted toward the terrified child. It was a little girl, they could see now. She was lying face down on the hard, hot blacktop, where she had stumbled and fallen in the left-hand lane.

Oh, no! Suzanne screamed in her mind. She reached the child a second ahead of her brother—in one, smooth move scooping up the tiny body, barely even breaking stride. Obviously in pain and desperate to escape, the child shrieked at the top of her lungs, flailing her arms and legs.

"*Look out!*" Tom yelled. A pickup screamed past at high speed, veering around them with its horn blaring, passing so close—*So close!*—that a burst of driven air thrust hard against them, pushing the twins off-balance and blowing their hair and clothes awry. Time seemed to stop as the pickup swerved to avoid their car parked in the middle of the road—then Suzanne spun about and bolted for the shelter of their vehicle. Tom scrambled right behind, guarding her back before she leapt into the front passenger seat, grasping the squirming, screaming child tight with both arms.

Tom flung himself into the driver's side, yanking the door closed as he edged the car off the highway, halting inches from the canyon wall. A cargo truck shot around the bend and tilted toward them, ripping by in the left lane. Behind it followed a slew of other vehicles, each passing with a deafening *whoosh* that rocked the Chevy.

Suzanne closed her eyes and took a deep breath. Her hands were shaking, and she felt hot and clammy. The sound of the pickup replayed in her mind, its horn drowning out the child's sobs. "He almost hit us," Suzanne whispered, shuddering.

Tom nodded grimly, but there was no time to waste. They had to escape the narrow passage between the canyon walls. He raised his voice above the wailing child. "We need to get out of here!"

He drove a few hundred yards north, beyond the cliffs and into open country, before pulling over to the right, off the blacktop and onto gravel that crunched under the tires.

"Whoa," he said, looking over at the little girl. It was difficult to wrap his mind around what had just happened. "One second everything's great, and then…" Country music still blared out of the car's speakers, like an echo from the past. Tom leaned forward and smacked the off button.

Suzanne continued to grasp the child with both arms, turning to gain eye contact without success. Tears poured down the sobbing girl's cheeks. "What's your name?" Suzanne whispered urgently. "Where are your mommy and daddy? And what are you *doing* out here all by yourself?"

The twins' summer plans—and those of their best friends, Pete and Kathy—had just taken an unexpected, life-changing detour. The little girl had wandered onto the highway and into their lives.

Nothing would ever be the same again.

2

A MYSTERY CHILD

"Look, she quite ignores me," Suzanne said, glancing at her brother with a wry half smile.

The little girl wore a beige sleeveless top, shorts, and tiny sandals. She cried and squirmed, refusing to talk or even glance at the two strangers who had just rescued—or captured—her. Blood oozed from cuts on both knees and the palms of her hands were scraped.

"Maybe she speaks Spanish," Tom offered.

The twins both spoke better-than-average high-school Spanish. Neither one had the chance to use the language much, but their grades had always been decent.

"¿Cuál es tu nombre?" Suzanne asked gently. "¿Dónde están tu mamá y papá?" No response. The girl, scared witless, studiously avoided the twins. She was filthy, her scratched arms and legs hot to the touch. Suzanne dabbed her knees with a tissue, forcing more screams.

Tom plugged his ears while his sister searched for a bottle of water in her purse. The sobbing girl grew calmer as she drank, drenching her top as the liquid spilled down.

"Where did she come from?" Suzanne wondered out loud.

"There's *nothing* out here."

"And nobody," Tom replied. "But someone must miss her." He honked the horn off and on, but no one appeared. Alone on the deserted highway, the little girl had escaped injury or even death by mere seconds.

"Let's call Dad," Suzanne suggested. With one arm wrapped around the child, she reached into her purse with her free hand for her cell phone. She touched her father's emergency number and hit speaker. The Chief, recognizing his daughter's number, answered on the first ring. The story tumbled out in a rush.

"Where are you?"

Tom answered. "Just south of Apache Canyon Drive, parked on the east side of Highway 89."

"Hold on for a second."

They listened as their father ordered a patrol officer to come to their aid. The little girl's halting sobs slowed.

"Is the child hurt?" the Chief asked, returning to his phone.

"Her knees are bleeding, but nothing serious. Scratched up, for sure." Suzanne giggled. "She's playing with the buttons on the dash."

"How old do you think she is?"

"Four or five."

Sudden movement in his rearview mirror drew Tom's attention. A black van that had passed them seconds before had pulled an abrupt U-turn and parked only a dozen yards behind them.

Despite the van's shaded front windshield, Tom observed a man with a huge head and a jowly, seamed face at the wheel. Dark, stringy hair hung down across his forehead, touching his sunglasses which, weirdly enough, looked too small for his face. The man leaned over his dash, stared above the shades, and scowled at the twins.

"Check this guy out, Suzie."

She turned, her eyes darting through the rear window. The intensity of the man's expression made her nervous. "Dad, a scary guy in a black van just parked right behind us. He's sitting there glaring—the guy's freaking me out."

Tom said, "He might know something about the little girl. Don't worry—I'll handle it."

"An officer should be there any minute," the Chief said, concern slipping into his voice.

Tom opened the driver's side door and stepped onto the blacktop just as a siren wailed in the distance. The van driver molded his hand into the shape of an imaginary revolver, pointed it at Tom, and pulled the imaginary trigger. Then he did the same to Suzanne. Her blood boiled. *This guy is a creep! Dangerous too.*

The driver goosed the van, shooting past the Chevy, narrowly missing Tom before roaring off at high speed.

"See," Tom said, chuckling nervously as he looked back at his sister. "I told you."

Suzanne rolled her eyes and hid the emotion in her voice. "He's gone, Dad, heading north. But the man was a lunatic. I don't think he had anything to do with this child."

"Got it. I alerted the Yavapai County Sheriff's Office. You're in their jurisdiction."

"Okay."

"I'll call your mother. She'll find a family to shelter the little girl."

After the birth of her twins, their mother, Sherri—a social worker for Yavapai County—had accepted a part-time position working from home. She often worked with displaced children.

The sound of the siren intensified with every passing second, dying away as a Prescott City Police cruiser pulled in behind the Chevy, red lights flashing. An eerie silence descended along the highway. The twins relaxed. Traffic slowed as people rubbernecked and crawled past them. Their new little friend seemed to sense a change. Suzanne held a tissue up to her nose, and the little girl gave it a good blow.

"One of your officers just arrived, Dad."

"That's Officer Kurt Jenkins. You'll be fine."

Two deputies from Yavapai County followed. An extensive search along both sides of the highway turned up empty. Tom trailed beside a deputy, excited to share in the action. Whomever

9

the little girl was—or where she came from—remained a mystery. The child didn't show up on the Lost or Missing Persons checklist, either.

"My guess is that someone dropped her off at the side of the road," Officer Jenkins said, rubbing his neck. "The scrapes are from her fall. Still, that doesn't explain those scratches. Could be a sign of neglect, even abuse."

"A man in a black van parked behind us," Suzanne said. "He acted crazy and sped off that way"—she pointed north—"just before you arrived."

"You're being overly dramatic," Tom said.

"You're kidding, right? What *he* did was dramatic. He made a gun shape with his hand and pretended to shoot us. Only lunatics do things like that."

"Yeah, your dad mentioned him," the officer shrugged. "According to your description, he drove away in the same direction I was traveling, so I didn't see his vehicle. Better let the deputies know. No license plate number?"

Tom shook his head no, vowing inwardly never to fail to note another license plate number. Then he called Ray Huntley, apologizing for missing an important club meeting. "No problem," Ray said. "Wow, I hope you find her parents."

Kathy called, worried that her best girlfriend hadn't shown up for their shopping trip. Suzanne apologized and explained what had happened.

"You've—got—to—be—kidding!"

"I wish. I'll call you later."

Other vehicles arrived, one after another, including a television mobile unit. Heidi Hoover, a reporter from *The Daily Pilot*, Prescott's hometown newspaper, had picked up the story from police radio frequencies. The star reporter had been the editor-in-chief of Prescott High's student newspaper in her senior year—just as the twins and the Brunellis were beginning junior high. They barely knew Heidi, but they had admired her from afar in school—

her parents were refugees from civil war in Mozambique, arriving in Prescott when Heidi was a small child.

"You're Suzanne, right?" Heidi asked with a big smile, extending her hand. "And is this your brother?" The three talked.

"They all want an interview," Suzanne said to Officer Jenkins minutes later. "With us. Talk about feeling embarrassed!"

"Don't be," the officer replied. "People love hero stories." Suzanne felt her face flush red.

Soon, Sherri arrived to take charge of the mystery child. It turned out the twins had been correct—the little girl was Spanish-speaking. Like many other Arizona social workers, she spoke the language fluently. Although the child refused to engage Sherri, it was obvious she understood.

A few minutes later, Sherri briefed the officers. "She's traumatized and refuses to talk. I couldn't get a word out of her. It took time before I could establish eye contact with her, but we're heading in the right direction. She understands Spanish, that's for sure. I asked her where her mommy and daddy are, and huge tears fell down her cheeks."

The child was starving. Sherri had brought food, and the silent girl happily munched on a slice of bread with peanut butter. "Suzie, she's so tiny," her mother said, sitting in the front seat of her car. The dark-haired child sat between them, quite content. "And look at those beautiful brown eyes."

"What happens now?" Suzanne asked.

"Well, she's traumatized, there's no doubt of that," Sherri replied. "I could place her with another family… but that might stress her out more. I think she should stay with us for a few days until we figure what's what."

Ecstatic, Suzanne gave her mother a hug. "Oh, wow, that's *great*. Did you hear, sweetie? You're coming to our home."

A little later, as things were wrapping up, Tom took his sister aside. "Suzie, you know what? This is awesome." He paused, his mind racing. His voice dropped lower, almost as if he were sharing a secret. *"This could be our first mystery."*

3

SCARY NEIGHBORS

"I 'll grab the paper!" Tom shouted as he tackled the stairs two at a time.

Still keyed up from the day before, he stepped outside, picked up Tuesday's edition of *The Daily Pilot* from the driveway and raced back into the house. "Suzie, check this out! You won't believe it."

His sister rushed downstairs. Tom had spread the front page across the kitchen table.

"Good grief," Suzanne muttered as her parents crowded around the twins. "Why is this such a big deal? Anybody would have done the same thing."

The headline read "Local teens save mystery child." Included was a close-up photo of the little girl's face. A smaller shot pictured the twins talking with the deputies.

"Well, you were there," her father said. "If it weren't for you two..." He didn't have to finish the sentence.

Sherri hugged them. "We're proud of you both."

"What an awful picture!" Suzanne grumbled. She tossed her head, pointing at the photo. Channel 5 had covered the story the evening before on the ten o'clock news. That was bad enough. This was worse.

Just then Kathy messaged her: *Congrats! Read the Pilot! U 2 r the best!*

"Okay, that's it." Suzanne grimaced. Her face turned bright red. "This is getting ridiculous."

"Getting?" her brother said, just to bug her.

"Who asked you, hotshot?" She kicked her brother under the table.

Tom ignored her. "Dad, what are the next steps for the Sheriff's Office?"

The Chief, dressed in uniform and ready for work, finished the last of his coffee. He didn't sound hopeful.

"Well, with a little help from you, the deputies checked out the surrounding countryside. There isn't a single clue pointing to her identity, and she's not listed as lost or missing. They've added her photo to the nationwide database for abandoned children, but that's about it." He paused. "Plus, summer is upon us. The sheriff is a little short of manpower—it's vacation time."

"No way will they ever find her family," Suzanne said, concern crossing her face. "That is tragic."

The twins' mother spotted movement by the kitchen entrance-way. "Look," she whispered. "We've got company."

Sherri stood up and walked over. The little girl had woken from a long sleep and followed their voices downstairs. Now she stood hiding around a corner just outside the kitchen, her eyes averted.

"Buenos días, cariña. Come and give me a big hug." Sherri picked the child up and cradled her. The whole family made a fuss out of her. Soon she was downing a bowl of cereal and eyeing the toast. Still, not a word crossed her lips.

Tom had an idea. "What if we showed her picture to the local ranchers? Maybe one of them knows something."

Suzanne brightened. *"Super* thought. We can find the time. Kathy and Pete will help too."

Neither twin doubted for a moment that their best friends would pitch in. The four high-schoolers, inseparable since their early years at St. Francis Elementary School, shared common values and many of the same interests.

The child's plight had touched the whole family. "I like it," their father said. He knew of the twins' fascination with mysteries. In fact, he encouraged it.

"Yes, it's well worth trying," their mother agreed with a smile. Sherri had a thing about discouraging anyone. Her positive attitude rubbed off on everyone.

"I'm off to work. Keep me informed." Chief Jackson kissed his wife goodbye and headed out through the garage.

The twins gobbled down their breakfast and called their friends. Tom logged on to Yavapai County's property tax website. He downloaded a list of every ranch owner within a three-mile radius of the intersection of Highway 89 and Apache Canyon Drive.

Next, he scanned the child's close-up from the newspaper and printed thirty copies of a flyer he created on his computer. Under a large picture of the little girl appeared the following captions:

I AM SEARCHING FOR MY FAMILY.
DO YOU KNOW ME?

ESTOY BUSCANDO A MI FAMILIA.
¿ME CONOCES?

THE TEXT BELOW AIMED TO TUG AT PEOPLE'S HEARTSTRINGS, retelling the story of a forlorn, deserted child found roaming along Highway 89—right in Prescott's own back yard, but outside its city limits. Tom included Suzanne's cell phone number as the contact information. "I have more time," she said. "Send the calls my way."

They took turns proofreading their Spanish translation, hoping they had everything right.

Soon enough Pete and Kathy arrived, eager to meet the new guest. The little girl turned shy once more, cuddling with Sherri and observing the excited group out of the corners of her eyes.

"It's like having four giants in the house," Sherri said, greeting the Brunellis with a warm smile.

The four friends high-fived one another, ready to dive into their first real-life case.

"You know what?" Pete asked. "This search is what plain-clothes police officers do."

"You're right—for a change," his sister agreed.

"Yeah," Pete said, ignoring his sister's dig. "We're, like, four —*mystery searchers.*"

Suzanne smiled. "Well, that's intriguing."

"Quite literally," Kathy said.

"I like it," Tom said. "Count me in."

With their coal-black hair and olive-hued skin, the Brunellis' Italian heritage was unmistakable. And they looked enough alike to be mistaken for twins. "Sometimes you can't even tell them apart!" the siblings' father, Joe, often said. Both were shorter and a little heavier than their tall, willowy friends.

Pete, a year older, was the impulsive one who moved too fast, talked too quickly, and enjoyed pushing the envelope. Occasionally, he paid the price. "Watch yourself," his father often counseled, "or one day you'll be in a world of hurt."

Kathy was a noisy, natural-born comic who could keep everyone laughing until their sides hurt. Her quick sense of humor was a gift from her mother, Maria, and one which Kathy effectively employed to cover up her life's biggest concern—her weight. *I'm a carbon copy of Mom in every way. And there's only one way to go.*

Their father, Joe, was an entrepreneur—the founder and editor of a popular national magazine that focused on world history. Maria, an emergency-room registered nurse, worked part-time at Prescott Regional Medical Center, the city's largest hospital.

The Brunelli siblings had driven over in their mother's car, so the four brand-new mystery searchers broke into pairs The boys agreed to handle Apache Canyon Drive on the west side of the highway while the girls scoured the east.

Tom set the plan in motion. "There are thirty ranches to cover. By splitting them up, we should be able to visit each one today."

"Show the flyer to every rancher," Suzanne said. "If no one's home, tape it to the front door."

"Ask questions," Tom suggested. "For example, 'Have you ever seen this little girl? Did you spot something unusual on 89 yesterday morning around 11:00 a.m.?'"

Pete nodded. "Okay, got it. Once we hear a yes to either question, we'll dig deeper. We might find a clue out there."

"In which case, you'll have one for a change!" Kathy quipped, poking her brother in the ribs. The two often sparred, but nothing ever really bothered Pete. Besides, he always got even with his sister —it was only a matter of time.

Tom called it. "Let's roll!"

4

———————————————

CANVASSING FOR CLUES

"We'll follow the girls," Pete prompted, "then split up at the intersection."

"Use our cell phones to stay in touch," said Suzanne. "If we hear something interesting, let's call each other."

"Okay!" The excitement level notched up higher.

Soon the two vehicles turned onto Apache Canyon Drive, the main east-west access road to every ranch in the area. Tom navigated while Pete drove west. Suzanne headed east as Kathy called out directions. Driving time from one ranch to the next was five minutes or less—the properties weren't far apart. Still, people often wanted to talk, making it difficult to end a conversation.

"Folks sure are friendly out here," Pete commented as he and Tom left the third ranch they visited.

But the girls were experiencing something far different.

"You're on private property!" yelled a grizzled old man. "*Get out of here!*"

The county map listed Neil Vanderbilt as the owner of an acreage that paralleled the east side of the highway. He stood, dusty and bedraggled, with shoulder-length grey hair, on the porch of a beat-up house that hadn't seen a paint job in decades. Worse, he cradled a shotgun in his arms. Two Rottweilers circled the Chevy, barking like crazy.

"*Yikes!* This guy is frightening, and so are his dogs," Kathy said. "At least he's not pointing that gun at us."

"Well, not *yet*," Suzanne snapped. Her voice had turned angry before she took a deep breath. "But we're not leaving without dropping off one of these." She opened her window an inch, slipped out a flyer and watched it flutter to the ground, making sure that Mr. Vanderbilt—or whoever the ugly guy was—had seen it and that it hadn't blown away

"Nice," Kathy said. "Very."

Once on their way again, the girls breathed easier. They drove back onto Apache Canyon Drive and headed north to the next ranch.

People who heard them knock or ring the bell always answered the door, but a handful of the residents weren't home. "Tape it up," Kathy said the first time that happened.

"This little girl will be famous," said Suzanne, using bits of masking tape to attach a flyer to a rancher's front door. "The whole countryside will know her story."

"Can't hurt."

One visit turned up a school acquaintance although neither of the girls had befriended her yet.

Their next stop was a smallish spread where towering cypress trees surrounded the ranch house and its attached double garage. A sizable cargo truck sat in the driveway. The house backed onto the highway, close enough that the girls noted the whine of passing traffic from the front porch. Kathy's knock brought Mike Lyons to the door, a stocky, soft-spoken man, dressed in jeans and a pullover, with a blotchy red face.

"Oh, sure," Mr. Lyons recalled. "I read the story in the paper this morning. Are you the ones who saved the little girl? I delivered packages along 89 yesterday—that's what I do; I'm a delivery driver. Never noticed a thing." He looked at them. "Say, what happened to the child, anyway?"

Suzanne gazed at Mr. Lyons's truck with a touch of anxiety. *Wow, it's just like the one that passed us on the highway.*

Meanwhile, the boys had run into a snag.

Posted on the electric security gates of two ranches were NO TRESPASSING signs. Yavapai County's property website listed the first one as vacant.

"No telling if it's deserted or not," Pete said as he surveyed the land. A new-looking late-model vehicle was parked out front, but junked cars rusted in the weeds.

"Tape the flyer to the gate," Tom said. "Where to now?"

The next acreage belonged to Parker Hall. His ranch, larger than any of the others that the boys had visited, ran south along Highway 89 for half a mile. Multiple buildings squatted behind the main house, including an open garage with two cars, plus a big red barn— all visible from the property's front gate. A circular driveway fronted the residence. Parked by the front door was a black van.

"Hey, remember him?" Pete blurted out, pointing to the listing. "He owns Hall's Hardware."

"Sure," Tom said. "My family has known him forever. Dad says Mr. Hall is the friendliest guy in town."

Pete snorted out loud. "You think? Check out the signage."

Attached to the closed gate appeared a red-lettered NO TRES-PASSING sign, flanked by a metal signboard peppered with shotgun pellets. It read: WE SHOOT FIRST, ASK QUESTIONS LATER.

A puzzled look crossed Tom's face. "He means business. That sure isn't like the Mr. Hall we know."

"Someone's coming from the house."

A heavyset, middle-aged man lumbered toward the gate, bare-headed and sweating, his eyes hidden by sunglasses. His hair fell down his forehead in sweaty clumps. "Can I help you?" he yelled.

Tom did a double take. *Could it be?* His eyes flickered over to the black van, but the man showed no sign of recognition.

The boys stepped out of the car and stood beside an industrial garbage bin. They reached across the gate to shake hands and introduce themselves.

The rancher told them his name was Hank Pauley. "I'm renting the ranch from Parker Hall," he offered.

Pete passed him a flyer, explaining the reason for their visit.

Mr. Pauley shook his head. "I drove along the highway yesterday morning, but never spotted a thing. It's a sad story."

The two friends chatted with him for another minute before saying goodbye and heading back to Pete's car. The rancher turned around and ambled back toward the house.

Tom spoke up in a hushed voice. "Hey, check out the top of the wooden telephone pole."

"The overhead light?" Pete asked. "Oh, wow, a security camera. No freaking way! It's turning, following us."

Tom glanced at Pete. "Someone's watching us. Right now. That is weird."

"Seriously weird," Pete said. "You know what? That guy has one of the biggest heads I've ever seen."

A light clicked in Tom's mind. Any shred of doubt had just evaporated. "You're right. I've seen—" His cell phone rang.

It was Suzanne. "How are you guys doing?" she asked. "We're wrapping up here." She filled the boys in on Neil Vanderbilt. "Aside from one mean old guy, we have nothing to report. Except both of us are starving."

"Drive in, knock on doors, shake hands, explain the story, leave flyer, wave bye-bye, drive away," Kathy singsonged in the background.

"Same here," Tom said to his sister, "with one exception so far. We still have two ranches on our list. Can we meet at the Shake Shop?"

Forty-five minutes later the boys drove up to the foursome's favorite go-to meeting place, since junior high. The girls sat on a picnic bench outside, enjoying the shop's famous icy-cold chocolate shakes.

Soon, munching on burgers and fries—"Hold the fries," Kathy said mournfully—the foursome compared notes.

"That guy scared the heck out of me," Suzanne said. "And his dogs were worse."

"Rattled me right out," Kathy nodded in agreement.

The big news from the west side of the highway was Hank Pauley. The boys discussed his mysterious and unnerving security camera.

"It's a strange feeling when people are watching you for no reason," Tom said.

"It was eerie," Pete said between bites. "Another thing too. He had the biggest head I've ever seen."

Suzanne stopped eating. "You're kidding, right?"

"No, I'm not. Huge."

"Did you see a black van?"

Tom broke the news. "He, uh. . . yeah, he had a black van. That was the exception I mentioned, Suzie. It was the same guy, no doubt."

"I can't believe it!" Suzanne said, setting the burger down on her plate.

"What's the matter?" Kathy asked.

Suzanne could close her eyes and replay the scene, so real and so vivid, seared into her memory: the roaring pickup, a lost and endangered little girl on her lap, a large cargo truck buffeting the Chevy, and then—minutes later—the sinister man with a huge head scowling at them.

She explained. "Then he cocked his hand in the shape of an imaginary revolver and pulled the imitation trigger—twice." The Brunelli's emitted a gasp. "But hotshot here doesn't think the guy is the least bit scary," Suzanne added, shooting her brother a look.

"He's nothing more than a harmless whacko," Tom said.

"We don't know that," his sister protested.

"We don't know otherwise."

Pete said, "Well, it sure *sounds* like the same guy. If Pauley is the one who parked behind you on 89, it's possible he spotted the kid in the car too."

"Creeps me out," Kathy said.

Suzanne's cell phone rang. She dug around inside her purse and glanced at the screen. "Hello?" *Click.* The line went dead. "That's funny. It said, 'Unknown Caller.' Then it disconnected."

A similar thought crossed their minds, but Kathy said it first, pumping her arm in the air. "The flyer worked. We're onto someone."

"Or," Pete said, "someone's onto *us!*"

5

RED FLAGS AT HALL'S HARDWARE

Suzanne woke her brother early on Wednesday morning and rushed downstairs. "It's our only chance," she insisted. "He's leaving for work in a few minutes."

Chief Jackson and his detectives had worked late into the night on a breaking case. This was the twins' first opportunity to debrief their father and they quickly filled him in.

"Dad," Tom concluded, "running into the guy with a huge head and a black van was too much of a coincidence."

"And the security camera," Suzanne added. "Isn't that suspicious?"

"Okay, you're assuming Hank Pauley and the man from 89 are one and the same. And it sounds more than possible," the Chief plunged ahead. "His ranch is close to where you found our little guest, but lots of people have big heads." He grinned and downed his coffee. "As for security cameras, they're common everywhere. Heck, Mr. Otto has one across the street. Think about it. Nothing connects this guy to the child—not yet, anyway. Plus, an individual parking behind you on the highway isn't necessarily significant. Neither is owning a black van."

"What about when he pretended to shoot us?" Suzanne asked.

"He was warning you away," the Chief replied. "For some unknown reason, he didn't want you stopping out there. His action was ugly but not illegal. Could be he's a little paranoid. Nothing we can do about that."

Gloom settled over the twins.

"Suzie," the Chief asked, "would you recognize him again?"

"Oh, for sure."

"Tom, you're sure it's the same guy?"

"One hundred percent."

"So let's confirm it with another set of eyes. Why not drive past the ranch a couple times? Suzie, see if you can spot him. Just don't be too obvious about it."

"Okay," Suzanne said, her spirits reviving.

"What if we talk with Mr. Hall at the hardware store?" Tom suggested. "He rented the property to Hank Pauley. He must know the guy."

The Chief agreed. "Sure. Do that first. Take a flyer with you. Gives you an excuse to visit him."

Suzanne's cell phone rang. She ran upstairs, returning seconds later. The caller had disconnected. "Dad, it's Unknown Caller again. Do you think it's the same person?"

"Could be," the Chief said. He stood, getting ready to leave. "Perhaps he knows something, but he's scared. You answer, but he can't force himself to talk. I've seen that before. More than once."

Sherri padded into the kitchen, holding the little girl in her arms. "We have a secret we want to share, don't we, Angelina?" The child buried her face into Sherri's shoulder, her beautiful brown eyes closed tight.

"¿Te llamas Angelina? Is that your name, sweetie?" Suzanne asked. "That is a pretty one. ¡Que linda!"

"Sure is," Sherri replied. "I went to get her for breakfast. She sat right up in bed and said, 'Me llamo Angelina.'"

"Does she know her last name?" Tom asked.

"We haven't figured that out yet, have we?" Sherri hugged Angelina.

Five minutes later the Brunellis messaged their friends: *Booked until midafternoon.* The Jacksons were on their own.

After washing dishes and helping to clean up, the twins drove out to Whiskey Row, Prescott's historic downtown section, dating back to 1900. Hall's Hardware, a corner store on Cortez Street, had been in the same building for more than a century. Summer visitors were flooding in and the area was hopping. Finding a parking place proved difficult.

"Circle the block a few times," Suzanne advised. "People are coming and going."

On their second drive-by, she noticed something extraordinary. "Whoa! Can you believe it?" Parked behind the hardware store, tight up against the building, was a black van.

Tom thought a moment. "Hank Pauley is renting the ranch from Mr. Hall. Why shouldn't he be here? Besides, black vans are common. Let's not jump to conclusions."

Suzanne needed convincing. "What if he's in the store?"

"We've got a great excuse for being here," Tom replied. "There's no reason to worry."

She gave her brother a withering look. "Who's worried?"

A parking spot opened. Soon they were pushing through the front door of Hall's Hardware and greeted by a pungent smell of old wood, fertilizer, and chemicals. Quiet music played in the background. The twins noted two clerks and a handful of customers. They didn't recognize a soul.

Tom approached a clerk. "Is Mr. Hall in this morning?"

"Sure," the man replied. "He's out back. I'll get him for you."

Soon, a smiling Parker Hall bustled toward them. A gentleman in his late sixties and on the shorter side, Mr. Hall wore a collared polo shirt and sported an old-fashioned small-brimmed straw hat that covered most of his white hair. He seemed to move in rapid motion all the time. He even talked fast. "Hey, it's the twins!" he called out, looking up to them. "Welcome. How are you both doing? Say, *excellent job* on saving that little girl out there on 89."

Mr. Hall's well-earned reputation for friendliness showed.

Suzanne blushed. "Oh, thanks, Mr. Hall. Anyone would have done the same thing."

He congratulated them again, shaking hands with both. "But it wasn't just anyone, it was you two, and I'm glad. Now, how can I help?"

"Well," Tom began, "her name is Angelina and we've been trying to find her family. We canvassed the ranches out there near the canyon, delivering flyers. Since you weren't around, we brought a copy for you."

"Why thanks, mighty nice of you," Mr. Hall said, studying the flyer. "I saw this picture in yesterday's newspaper."

"Yup, she told our mom her name is Angelina. We dropped one of these off with Hank Pauley." The twins watched Mr. Hall's reaction.

"Sure, Hank rents the ranch from me. Was he able to help?"

"Nope, said he hadn't seen a thing," Tom replied.

"Sorry, me neither. I haven't visited the old homestead in months. Pauley lives there with his cousin and their families. I'm told they keep it real neat."

"It's in great shape," Tom said. "There's even a security camera at the gate."

"No kidding? Well, you can't be too careful nowadays. I'm sure he's trying to protect his cattle."

"Mr. Pauley, uh, didn't say much," Tom said, searching for words, "so we wanted to—"

Suzanne finished her brother's sentence, blushing once more. "—ask if you felt he was a good man, reliable… that sort of thing."

"Oh, yes," Mr. Hall said. "I haven't seen Pauley for weeks, but I'm told he's polite and gets along with the neighbors. Plus, he pays his rent on time. Always a good sign." He chuckled. "Altogether, I'd say the man's a solid citizen."

After more chitchat, the twins bid goodbye and returned to the car.

"Tom, we need to watch the back of the store. If Parker Hall hasn't seen Hank Pauley for weeks, who the heck is driving that van?"

"Could be a different one."

"I doubt it."

"You never know."

Parking was still close to impossible. They circled the block twice before another vehicle pulled out from the curb.

"Perfect view." Tom nosed into the space, glancing toward the store. The van hadn't moved. They waited. Ten minutes passed. Twenty.

The rear door of Hall's Hardware flew open. A large man stepped out, tiny sunglasses hiding his eyes. It was easy to see he had a huge head topped with black, scraggly hair.

"*Look*," whispered Suzanne, astonished. "That *is* him! He's the one who parked behind us on the highway. The creep who pretended to shoot us!"

"Yup, it's the same guy—Hank Pauley," Tom said. "I'd recognize him anywhere."

Just then, Mr. Hall stepped out on to the sidewalk, clearly not his usual mild-mannered, jovial self. He seemed to be yelling at Pauley, and his arms were flailing around. He shook his fist in the air.

"Look," Suzanne said. "Mr. Hall's not happy about something, that's for sure. This isn't good. I think the big guy's dangerous."

"They *both* lied to us," Tom said. "Mr. Hall said he hadn't seen Pauley in months. Why? The whole thing is beyond kooky."

"How are they connected to Angelina? I don't get it."

"Once we solve that riddle, we'll know why she was wandering along the highway by herself."

Early in the afternoon, the four friends met at the Jacksons'. The twins' unsettling experience at Hall's Hardware tumbled out.

"No way!" the Brunellis chorused.

"Mr. Hall fibbed," Tom said. "That means they're hiding something."

"Yeah, but what?" Pete wondered out loud.

Suzanne asked, "And what to do now? That big guy is too creepy for words."

Kathy said, "What are our options?"

Silence.

Pete broke the spell. "Maybe we should talk to the neighbors."

"I dunno," Tom replied cautiously. "We'd tip off Pauley. He doesn't want us poking around, that's for sure. And now he's on guard." He focused. "But I do have one idea."

6

FLIGHT INTO DANGER

A year earlier, Prescott High's technology club had built a compact, lightweight ultra-quiet drone equipped with a miniature camera.

"From a kit," Tom said, relishing the memory. "The thing is *amazing*."

Suzanne agreed. "Fast too."

The handheld controller captured live video footage or still images, which were also viewable on any smart wireless device connected to it. Tom, the club's team leader, had learned to fly the drone to record school events. Suzanne had pitched in too, piloting more than once. Now Tom proposed an unusual use for the miniature aircraft.

"I knew what you were thinking," his sister said. "I hope we're not getting ourselves into trouble."

Tom defended his idea. "No way, Suzie. This might be our best shot. We only need one telltale clue."

Pete was eager, but doubtful. "If there's something strange going on, you can count on it being well hidden."

"Get ready for a boring flyby," Kathy said. "I'll bet we see nothing but cattle and hay."

"You never know," Suzanne said.

Ray Huntley, the technology club president, returned Tom's phone call within the hour. Although he was cautious about lending out the club's gear for use off-campus, Ray knew and trusted Tom.

"Sure, okay, no problem," he said, after a moment's hesitation. "What's the purpose?"

"A video survey. I only need it for two days."

"Okay. Just bring it back in one piece."

An hour later, the twins picked up the drone and drove straight to Prescott High's empty grounds. The Brunellis, lounging on the grassy field, had beat their friends by a few minutes. After preparing the miniature aircraft for flight, it took only seconds to reach a cruising altitude of four hundred feet, the maximum height allowed by U.S. federal law. The onboard HD camera captured a live video stream of the surrounding area, feeding it to an app on Pete's cell phone. Everything ran without a hitch.

"Whoa, you were right. This thing *is* fast!" Pete said.

"No fooling," Kathy said. "Look at it soar."

They planned to deploy the next evening, just before sunset, around seven thirty.

Tom worked out the amount of air time required. "The entire flyby should last less than fifteen minutes, I hope."

"How visible is the drone from ground level?" Kathy asked.

"At a hundred feet, most people wouldn't even notice," he replied. "Plus, it's super quiet."

"All good," Pete said. "But I keep picturing that sign on the electric gate, 'We Shoot First, Ask Questions Later.'"

Tom groaned and rolled his eyes. "Don't even mention it."

ON THURSDAY MORNING AFTER BREAKFAST, THE BOYS SCOUTED THE country around Parker Hall's ranch, searching for a secret base from which to operate. As they drove past the gate, their focus of attention was on the security camera, trying to figure out the area covered by its range of motion. But the device was still: no movement, not a twitch. The van was there, the garage and barn doors shut tight.

"It's just too quiet," Pete said. "Didn't Mr. Hall tell you there were two families living out here? Where are the kids?"

Soon they spotted an old road overgrown with grass leading to a deserted homesite, across the main gravel roadway from Parker Hall's ranch and a few hundred yards farther south. Whatever had once been was long gone. A grove of trees surrounded the empty site on three sides.

"This is perfect," Tom said. "Nothing here but wind and trees."

Pete lauded the site too. "Couldn't be better. We'll park the car on the other side of the grove. You'd never see it from the road."

"Yup, it's a great spot for launching," Tom said.

THE BRUNELLIS ARRIVED AT THE JACKSONS' HOUSE SHARP AT 6:00 p.m., and the foursome reviewed their evening strategy. Then the boys headed out, driving out to the hidden homesite.

"If the security camera shows any movement, we'll cancel for tonight and try again tomorrow," Tom said.

Suzanne and Kathy cruised out to the intersection of Apache Canyon Drive and Highway 89. A restaurant occupied the northeast corner. The two friends hid in its parking lot, wearing sunglasses as they faced west. A blinding sun was setting in glorious Arizona colors.

If something went wrong, it was their job to distract the bad guys.

"Hey, if you need us, we're a minute away," Suzanne said.

Kathy chimed in brightly. "One call and we'll come to your rescue."

As the boys drove past the ranch, the security camera didn't stir. Still, they thought it likely that the device was auto-capturing images. Pete zipped past—the black van sat out front while two cars parked in the open garage. Someone had closed the barn door.

Pete nosed into the deserted homesite, hiding the car behind the trees. Soon the drone rested on the grassy road, ready for action. The sun was still setting as they counted down the minutes.

At seven thirty, right on schedule, Pete gave out a whoop. "Let her fly!"

"It's off!" Tom cheered.

With a slight whirring sound, the drone lifted into the air and soared straight up, climbing to one hundred feet. It wasn't much more visible than a bird in the sky.

Pete monitored the action on his cell phone. "Camera's live. Image is sharp. We still have enough light. Good angle of view."

Tom, operating the controller, could see everything on-screen too. Meanwhile, across the highway, the girls' cell phone screens flickered to life.

"The drone's right above the road," Kathy said. "Let's hope it never crosses over onto their land." They all knew that U.S. law prohibits flying a drone over someone's private property without permission.

The aircraft surveyed the ranch from a network of roads that ran along three sides of the ranch. The highway bordered the fourth. As it passed over the intersection, the girls jumped out of the car and gazed skyward, searching in the waning light.

"I can't see it," Suzanne said.

Kathy laughed. "Darn good thing."

So far, the video stream showed no signs of life. No people, no children playing, no dogs. Nothing.

"A cattle ranch with no cattle," Pete said. "Now that is strange. There isn't a steer in sight."

Tom whistled. "Wow, you're right."

Suzanne picked up on it too. "One more fib from Mr. Hall," she said, almost whispering to herself.

"I'll bet that big guy ate 'em all!" Kathy quipped.

"Or maybe Mr. Hall has never been out to see the ranch since he rented it to his new tenant, and it's Pauley who lied to *him* about keeping cattle there," Suzanne added.

Behind the barn and a hundred yards farther out, a surprise appeared in the dimming light. "Check it out!" Pete yelled. A helicopter sat on a recessed landing pad.

"Whoa," Kathy said. "Imagine that. How many ranches have a helicopter?"

"Or a landing pad?" Suzanne parried.

Tom dropped the miniature aircraft lower and swooped around the canary-yellow copter. There wasn't a soul anywhere.

Within minutes, the drone had finished its 360-degree survey. Tom piloted it to a hundred feet above the main gate, hovering high, its camera lens centered on the barn behind the ranch house.

"Hey," Tom said, his voice notching up. "Another vehicle just pulled onto the ranch."

"Who's this guy?" Pete asked.

A dark late-model sedan appeared on their screens, bumping along the dirt road before coming to rest beside the black van. The driver stepped out of the car. Tom dropped the drone twenty-five feet to get a better view.

The barn's front door swung wide open. It was getting dark, but the distinctive blue-white light of monitor screens poured out, illuminating Hank Pauley as he walked toward the newcomer. Deep in the barn, two other men sat before giant computer screens, tapping the glowing surfaces with their fingers.

"*What's going on in there?*" Tom asked, his eyes glued to the screen.

"No clue," Pete replied. "Try for a straight-in shot of the barn's interior. Fly south a couple hundred feet."

"What are the computer guys doing?" Kathy asked, glancing at Suzanne with a look of amazement.

"Who knows," her best friend replied. "It's bizarre—not what you'd expect in the barn of a cattle ranch, that's for sure."

Tom sent the drone farther south while maintaining its view of the open barn doors. His screen said the machine was hovering at seventy-five feet.

Just then, Hank Pauley pointed toward the sky straight at the drone. The newcomer—an older man, appearing much smaller as he stood beside the heavyset rancher—spun around, both arms animated and flapping in the blue-white glow. The barn door slammed shut, the glowing light vanished. Pauley rushed to his van.

Pete felt his mouth go dry. "They spotted it. Tom! *Get the heck out of there!*"

Tom sent the aircraft winging north, away from the boys' secluded hideout. The surrounding countryside whipped by at high speed on everyone's screens.

Moments later, two rifle shots rang out in the falling darkness.

"They're shooting at it!" Tom shouted.

Pete's heartbeat raced. *"Go higher!"*

7

SAVED

Suzanne went pale. "*Gunshots*. They're after the drone. We're up!" She fired up the Chevy.

Kathy snapped her seat belt shut. "No fear."

Easier said than done.

On the other side of the highway, Pete said, "Uh-oh, they'll follow it back here. Make it disappear, now."

Sure enough, from their position on the deserted homesite, the boys could see vehicles moving at the ranch. Headlights cut into the deepening twilight as Tom piloted the machine up to four hundred feet.

The van and a second vehicle hesitated at the ranch's security gate, then rushed north.

"Okay, bring it on home," Pete urged. Within a minute the aircraft had landed on the grassy road, ten feet away from them.

"Great!" Tom yelled, running toward the drone.

"Never looked so good."

Kathy caught the action on her cell phone, describing the play-by-play scene for Suzanne: the drone coming in for a landing, bumping along the path before an abrupt stop. In the falling darkness, shadow movements danced across her screen as the boys sprinted over to it.

"They got it," Kathy exclaimed. Relief flooded over her.

"Super," Suzanne said, taking a deep breath. "Now let's hope the bad guys don't get them. We're almost there."

Meanwhile, the boys packed up the hardware, fast.

"Did we power off?" Pete asked.

"Yup. Careful," said Tom. "I'll box the controller and toss it in the backseat." The latches of the drone's case locked with a loud *snap!*

Pete's voice cracked with a touch of panic. "I bet they're tearing the country up looking for us."

The boys stored everything away, then jumped into the vehicle and slammed the doors shut. They opened the front passenger windows, sat back, and waited in nervous silence. Pitch black had enveloped the landscape.

"How the heck did they spot it?" Pete asked.

"The sun was still setting," Tom replied. "The drone must have caught a glint of the sun's last rays."

"And Pauley spotted it," Pete said. "Talk about bad luck for us."

Soon there was the roar of vehicles racing along Apache Canyon Drive. A van shot by on the gravel road before a late-model sedan turned into the old homesite. As he hammered the brakes, the driver flashed his high beams and illuminated the towering trees. A murky yellow cloud of dust floated upward, hazing the headlights.

At that moment the girls drove past, heading south—falling in behind the van without even realizing it. The driver of the sedan reacted, throwing his vehicle into reverse and swinging onto the road with a wide arc. He tore after the Chevy.

"It worked!" Kathy shrieked. "The other guy's right behind us."

Perfect. Lights out, windows open, the boys' car cruised out, quiet and unseen, turning right and racing off to the far side of the highway. The evidence of their misadventure sat tucked away on the backseat.

Tom struggled to wrap his mind around the crazy night. "They darn near caught us."

"Yup," Pete agreed, stretching out and twisting his neck to relieve the tension. "We spooked them. Now it's up to the girls."

Meanwhile, the van had pulled a U-turn. Half a mile down the road, Suzanne and Kathy found themselves boxed in, forced to a complete stop. Hank Pauley leaped out of his van and rushed over to Suzanne's side of the car. He bent over, his mouth almost touching the window, scowling at her with an intensity she had experienced only once before.

Suzanne shuddered. Despite her adventure on Highway 89, this was the first time she had come face to face with the sinister man. She cracked open her window—an inch.

"Someone fired a rifle out here. It wasn't you, was it?" he said, his voice threatening. Black, stringy hair hung down to his suspicious eyes. He was red-faced and his bad breath came in rasps. The other driver walked up from behind the Chevy, flashlight in hand, and surveyed the backseat of their car with a searching beam of light. Kathy watched as the man shook his head at Pauley before turning around and walking back to his sedan.

A tense Suzanne, thinking fast, kept her cool. "Nope, not us. We're looking for the Vanderbilt residence."

Kathy prayed her trepidation didn't show.

"That's the other side of the highway," Pauley said in a wooden voice, spitting the words through clenched teeth. He stared at Suzanne for a few more seconds, then shifted his intense gaze to Kathy, searching for something. *Anything*, she realized. She looked away but it was easy to see the heavyset man was more than skeptical. Without another word, he strode over to his car, never once glancing behind him The girls watched as the two vehicles raced off, spewing gravel behind them.

"*Whew.* Thank goodness he's out of here," Suzanne said, exhaling deeply.

"Great job, Suzie," Kathy said. Her fear dissipated as Pauley retreated into the night. They high-fived each other. "You were right. That guy is one scary dude. Imagine what would happen if they caught the boys." At that second her cell phone rang.

"Are you okay?" her worried brother asked.

"Yeah, we're fine. Suzie handled Hank Pauley like nothing I've ever seen. We'll tell you all about it. Did you guys get out of there?"

"You bet we did," Pete said. Then, a rare compliment popped out. "Thanks to you two."

"Don't mention it," Kathy said dryly. "We heard them shooting at the drone."

"Creeped us right out," Pete replied. "We're across the highway in the parking lot."

"On the way," Kathy said.

A couple minutes later the girls pulled up beside their brothers. They gave one another a thumbs-up, then trooped home to Prescott. An unusual silence filled the cabins of both cars. The four mystery searchers—each lost in his or her own thoughts—felt grateful to be alive, safe, and far, far away from the evil-seeming threat of Hank Pauley.

8

UNKNOWN CALLER

A clear, bright and crisp Friday morning dawned, promising another warm summer day.

The twins were dying to talk to the Chief, but he left before sunup. They drove out to Ray's and returned the drone, repacked and in one piece. "We're trying to solve the riddle of where Angelina came from," Suzanne explained to Ray.

"We used it to survey the surrounding country," Tom said. "So far, no answers."

Ray wished them the best of luck. "I sure hope you can find her family."

The afternoon featured a doubles tennis match and the boys tagged along to watch. The girls broke a losing streak, which encouraged Pete to tease his sister. "You got lucky."

"Perhaps, but I can beat you, no problem," she countered with her trademark smile.

"Anytime."

Later, after the girls had changed out of their tennis outfits, the four met to pursue their case. There was much to discuss.

"So you think it was the setting sun that caught us?" Kathy asked.

"Yeah, pretty sure," Tom replied. "Something tipped them off, and that's our best guess."

"That helicopter is a mystery," Pete said. "How do we find out who owns it—and who flies it?"

Suzanne frowned. "Somehow, I doubt it would be Pauley."

"Well," Tom said. "I'll bet the Federal Aviation Agency website could tell us lots." He pulled out his cell phone and scanned the video captured the night before. "Here's the identification number from the helicopter: N73T454.

Kathy jumped online too. Just minutes later she called out, "Got it!"

"You're kidding," Suzanne said.

"Not the pilot," she replied, "but the helicopter is a rental. It's a Bell Jetranger owned by Cooper Aviation in Phoenix."

"Okay," Pete said. "That could be a great clue. What's next?"

"Good question," Suzanne said. "We can't just go there and spy on them, right? They'll be on guard."

"No more drones, either," Kathy added. "Otherwise the bad guys might get lucky."

"Scary," Suzanne said. "Imagine them shooting at it—or *us!*"

AFTER DINNER THAT EVENING, THE FOURSOME GATHERED IN THE Jacksons' living room. The Chief joined them, but Sherri excused herself to help with a fundraising event. "I can't skip it. Maria is picking me up in a few minutes," she said.

"Good thing," Suzanne whispered. "Mom would freak out."

"Mine too," Kathy replied quietly.

The conversation circled back to Hall's Hardware.

"I can understand why Hank Pauley was there, but I can't figure out why Parker Hall lied," the Chief said. He had known the store owner since childhood.

The drone's video was next. No one uttered a word as the Chief leaned forward, taking in every second.

"I'm sure they thought the drone was over their property," he said, unfazed by the rifle shots. "People take potshots at those things all the time."

"But we didn't cross over their land!" Tom protested.

"I get it. But they perceived the drone as a threat. There's no doubt they were looking for whoever was controlling it. Having computer monitors in a barn isn't illegal. Maybe they're doing software development for a corporate client, and they need to keep the project confidential. Those monitors sure are huge."

The helicopter didn't surprise the Chief either. "They're into security—materials are being transported by air. That reduces the risk of a road accident or traffic stop, which could lead to embarrassing questions." He paused. "You realize their security camera must have captured pics of your cars, right?"

"Yeah," Tom admitted, "we figured that out."

"Well, I've got a good overall picture," the Chief said. "Now, how does Angelina fit into this?"

Collective silence.

Finally, Suzanne answered. "That is the million-dollar question we've discussed darn near every day. We can't imagine any connection between Angelina and Hank Pauley."

"Except that he parked behind you on 89 and gave you the evil eye," Kathy said.

"Worse than that," Suzanne said. "The lunatic pretended to shoot us."

"Well," the Chief responded, "*pretending* isn't a criminal act and proves nothing. Officer Jenkins could be right. Perhaps someone dropped Angelina off at the side of the highway."

That was a depressing thought. The four friends, looking crestfallen, fell silent again.

"Look, you must consider every possibility," the Chief hastened to add, realizing that he had deflated the team. "Don't give up yet. There's a shortage of leads, but that doesn't mean your investigation has hit a dead end. Put your heads together."

"Okay!" they shouted in unison.

"Two more things. Kathy, you recorded the license number of the guy who spotted the drone. Do you still have it?"

"You bet." She searched for a memo on her cell phone. "Arizona plates, Bl354667."

"Perfect," the Chief responded, writing it down. "Any idea what make of car he was driving?"

"It was a big four-door sedan," Kathy answered. "New. Might have been a Ford."

"Thank you."

"You're welcome," Kathy replied, feeling very pleased with herself.

"We captured the helicopter's ID number too," Tom said. "It showed up on the Federal Aviation Agency's website. It's a Bell Jetranger owned by Cooper Aviation in Phoenix."

"You might call them," the Chief advised. "Ask Cooper if that make and model is available for rent, or if they have it out on a long-term lease that might end soon. They'll think of you as a prospect, and that should get them talking."

The four mystery searchers felt pumped again.

Suzanne's cell phone rang. Her purse lay on the table in front of her. She dug inside it until she found her cell and glanced at the screen.

Kathy peeked over her shoulder. "Hey, it's your old buddy," she said.

Sure enough, Unknown Caller was back again. "Boy, he's a pest," Suzanne said, irritated.

"Let me try," said Kathy, reaching for the cell phone. "Hello?" She put the call on speaker.

"Who's this?" an older-sounding man's voice asked. Suzanne reacted, her head tilting back in surprise.

Kathy stood. "My name is Kathy. Who's calling?"

"I am," the man replied.

Kathy rolled her eyes at the others. "I know, sir. But who are you?"

"Are you one of the young ladies who came out to my ranch last week?" he demanded.

Kathy hesitated for a second or two. "Why yes, I—we—did," she replied, with no idea *what* ranch.

"This is Neil Vanderbilt. Get back here, soon—and *by yourselves!*" Then he disconnected.

The Chief stood up to leave, looking at the shocked team in amusement. "Well, there you go. I'd say your hard work has resulted in a promising new lead." He chuckled as he walked toward the garage. "It never pays to give up."

Then he turned and pointed toward the girls. "*Don't* go out there by yourselves. And just to be on the safe side, go out in daylight."

The door closed behind him.

9

A HIDDEN PLATFORM

Saturday morning, just after breakfast, the foursome gathered at the Brunellis'.

"That guy sounds like a real nut," Pete said. "Why is he insisting that you two 'young ladies' go out there by yourselves?"

"Something's up," Tom said. "And we don't know anything about him."

"Well, we can't *all* go out," Kathy said. "He'll turn hostile and refuse to talk. What if he knows something?"

After a brief discussion, it ended up that Kathy and Tom would make the trip together—right now. Instead of phoning first, they drove out to visit Neil Vanderbilt unannounced. But Tom had misgivings, nonetheless.

"This really does make more sense," Kathy said as she turned into Mr. Vanderbilt's ranch. "He might freak out if we had told him you were coming along instead of Suzanne. Remember, this time he extended an invitation."

"Not to *me*," Tom said.

"He'll get over it."

"I hope he told the dogs to expect guests."

"We're about to find out."

Sure enough, the two Rottweilers rushed out and circled the car, jumping and barking, as Kathy coasted up the driveway.

Neil Vanderbilt stepped out through his front door, still dusty and bedraggled. But today he wore a slight smile—until he spotted Tom. Mr. Vanderbilt froze for a few seconds before emitting a piercing whistle. The dogs turned around, dashed back to their master, and jumped onto the porch, tails wagging.

"First good sign," Kathy said.

"Better yet, he's not carrying a shotgun." Tom said, relieved.

Kathy pulled to a stop. The two stepped cautiously out of the car, keeping sharp eyes on the Rottweilers.

"Who's he?" Mr. Vanderbilt demanded, jabbing an index finger toward Tom. "I didn't invite him out here."

"This is my friend's brother," Kathy replied.

The man grumbled to himself.

"Are the dogs friendly?" Tom asked, trying not to show his nervousness.

"You'd know it if they weren't," Mr. Vanderbilt said. "Go ahead, boys!"

The Rottweilers leaped off the porch and bounded over to the two startled visitors, tails wagging and tongues whipping around. It turned out that the dogs—both black with large white patches from head to toe—were brothers: Bart and Blackie.

Tom knelt to pet one of the huge beasts. Bart rolled over on his back. "Hey, they *are* friendly."

"My new best friend," Kathy said, laughing as Blackie licked her hands nonstop, thumping his tail into the dirt.

The dogs were obviously Mr. Vanderbilt's pride and joy. "They're super watchdogs, scare the heck out of visitors and tres-passers. But I raised them as good critters."

Kathy and Tom introduced themselves and shook hands with the rancher. All the time he eyed Tom warily.

"I never imagined coming back here," Kathy said, studying Mr. Vanderbilt's face. "You scared us." Somehow the man had changed.

The gruff old guy looked the same, but his demeanor was different. A kinder, gentler version stood before them.

"Yeah, for personal reasons I don't want people out here. My privacy is very important."

Tom challenged him. "You called a few times anonymously—that made the girls nervous."

"Get over it. Making that call made *me* nervous. I knew it might complicate my life," he muttered.

Kathy held her breath. "Do you have something to tell us?"

"Follow me," he replied.

They trailed Mr. Vanderbilt to the back of his house as the dogs raced ahead. At the rear of the home, unseen from the front yard, was a curving staircase attached to the exterior wall that led to a two-story rooftop platform.

"C'mon up," he encouraged them, leading the way.

The platform afforded a 360-degree bird's-eye view of the surrounding ranch country. Apache Canyon Drive cut through the rolling hills and canyons on both sides of the highway. Vehicles were zipping up and down 89, and a single car slowed as it approached the intersection. Hues of green summer grass and trees in blossom dominated the countryside.

Kathy marveled at the scenic beauty. "It's like a picture postcard."

Parker Hall's ranch lay in a straight line across 89. They could make out the black van parked in the distance and two cars in the garage. The barn door appeared to be closed.

The platform offered plenty of room. Mr. Vanderbilt, Kathy, and Tom shared the space with both dogs. There was an easy chair for the rancher, plus full water bowls for the Rottweilers.

The centerpiece was a large telescope.

"Star gazing," Mr. Vanderbilt said, blinking in response to the curious expressions on his visitors' faces. "It's my hobby. If you don't mind," he added, sitting down, "I'll rest here. I feel older every day."

Then he leaned forward. His tone grew serious; his voice dropped lower.

"A week ago, a truck pulled into the ranch yonder. It was evening, before nine o'clock. Eight people got out, I counted them. Seven adults and one little girl. She was holding a woman's hand— her momma's, I thought. I looked at them"—he pointed to the giant telescope—"through that. They carried suitcases and headed straight for that double garage beside the house. It wasn't the first time. Folks come and go every few weeks. They appear to be transients. Nothing to do with me."

"Didn't the neighbors wonder?" Kathy asked. "I mean, that's unusual, right?"

Mr. Vanderbilt ignored her questions. "Later the next morning, we came up here, me and the dogs, to check things out. Around ten or eleven, I think. It was real overcast, with dark storm clouds. The same folks, looked like, were coming out from the garage. They climbed into the rear of the truck with their suitcases. The driver closed up and drove away."

He glanced at them both. "Guess who was missing?"

"Angelina," Kathy and Tom spoke nearly in unison.

Mr. Vanderbilt nodded. "Yup. The little girl. I didn't know her name—it wasn't on your flyer. But it was her, no doubt about it. I recognized the photo."

Kathy's heart sped faster. "Wasn't the whole thing a little odd to you?"

"Nope. It's none of my business. Never gave it another thought." He paused. "Until you showed up. Then it hit me. I felt sorry for that child."

"So, what happened, Mr. Vanderbilt? Why did they leave Angelina behind?" Tom asked.

He leaned forward again, as if sharing a secret. "Call me Neil. Well, I'm sure it wasn't on purpose. It's obvious the child spent a couple hours waiting for her momma. When Mom didn't show up, she musta snuck out and went looking for her. The highway isn't far from the ranch. That's when you all found her."

Kathy was aghast. "Poor Angelina. She was all alone, frightened to death I'm sure."

"Mr. Vanderbilt—Neil," Tom corrected himself, "did you ever talk to the property owner over there?"

"No idea who he is, and I don't care. I enjoy my privacy. Besides," he said, winking at them, "the dogs scare off everybody."

"Was the driver a big guy with a huge head?" Tom asked.

"Well, he's big, that's for sure, but I never noticed his head. He lives there. I've seen him in the past."

"Ever see other people out there?"

"Except for the transients? Not that I recall."

"Neil, could we view the ranch through your telescope?" Kathy asked.

He jumped up out of his easy chair. "Oh, help yourself. This thing is my baby. I'll show you how it works."

He focused on a parked car a mile north on the highway. "Line up the viewfinder and adjust it for your eyes. Go ahead, check it out."

The telescope's power was amazing. Kathy was first—she could clearly see the faces of people sitting in the vehicle, talking to each other. "That is something else. The night sky must be an experience."

"You bet. Greatest hobby in the world," he responded with a chuckle.

"Okay if I turn it toward the ranch?" Kathy asked.

"Be my guest. Just swing it around."

Kathy spun the telescope due west, pointing straight at Parker Hall's property. As she focused in, Hank Pauley walked out of his front door and headed for the van. His sinister face filled the viewfinder.

She frowned. "Look who's there."

Tom took a turn. "No surprise," he replied.

"What are you looking at?" Neil asked.

"Parker Hall's ranch."

"You mean that one, across the highway?"

"Yes. The guy driving away rents it."

"Well," said Neil, "I hate to mention this, but you're looking at the wrong ranch."

"What?" Kathy and Tom chorused, turning toward Neil in shock. "The wrong ranch?"

"Correct. Lemme show you."

Neil cranked the telescope forty-five degrees to the right and adjusted the scope. "Here, take a gander."

Kathy peered into the viewfinder before straightening. She recognized the ranch north of the Vanderbilt property, the one with the cypress trees around the house and a cargo truck parked in the front driveway.

"The neighbors wouldn't see a thing," she said. Tom's eyes darted to Kathy's ashen face before gazing into the viewfinder.

"You've got it," Neil said. "From this height, we can see everything. At ground level, there's no visibility unless you get past those trees."

Tom whistled. "Who lives there?" he asked. No one answered.

Kathy turned and locked eyes with the rancher. "You're telling us the little girl walked away from *Mike Lyons's* ranch?"

"I haven't the faintest idea who Mike Lyons is," Neil responded, pointing with his index finger, "but that's where Angelina came from!"

1 0

A NEW PLAN

W hile Tom and Kathy visited Mr. Vanderbilt, Suzanne and
Pete placed a call to Cooper Aviation.

"Okay, ready?" Suzanne asked. They had rehearsed their script several times.

"Let's do it."

An operator answered. "Good morning, Cooper Aviation. How many I help you?"

Pete led off. "We're interested in renting a Bell Jetranger. Do you have one available?"

"One minute, please. I'll connect you to Ken Curtis, our rentals manager."

As they expected, Mr. Curtis was more than curious about who the callers were and what their specific interest was.

"Well, we're researching helicopter rentals for my father," Suzanne answered, "and he's only interested in *that* model."

"Well," the manager replied, "I hate to disappoint you, but we just sold off our only Jetranger."

"Oh, really? If you don't mind me asking, what kind of client would opt for a Jetranger?"

"All kinds. We sold this one to Raydon Paper Company, in Scottsdale."

Suzanne's fingers tapped discreetly on her laptop keyboard.

Pete said, "Thanks, Mr. Curtis. We appreciate your time."

"No problem."

Moments passed before Suzanne piped up again. "Pete, you won't believe this."

"Try me."

"Raydon manufactures special paper for passports, banknotes, and bearer bonds. They provide security paper to governments around the world."

"You gotta be kidding!" Pete exclaimed. "Know what this means?"

"Sure. Someone's doing top-secret stuff out in Parker Hall's barn. We've stumbled onto something big."

THAT EVENING, THE TWO PAIRS OF MYSTERY SEARCHERS GATHERED TO debrief each other. The events of the day tumbled into the open.

"It looks like we're chasing a couple of different cases," Pete said.

"Both involve illegal activity," his sister noted. "Criminal, in fact."

"It's possible they're connected," Suzanne said. "Then again…"

"I've been thinking about something," Tom said quietly—always a sure sign that he was turning over an idea in his mind.

"Uh-oh," Kathy said with a sly smile.

"No, I'm serious," Tom continued. "Pete, remember the garbage bin at Parker Hall's ranch? The big industrial unit out front? It was beside the gate."

"Sure. We stood next to it when we met Hank Pauley."

"Right. Whatever they're doing requires the use of that huge bin, unusual for a ranching operation. If we could just remove a bag or two—"

"Hang on. You're forgetting the security camera," Suzanne said, grabbing her brother's arm. "Isn't that risky?"

54

"Hmm," Tom said. "Good point. How do we handle that?"

"Well…" Pete said, hesitating for a few seconds, "we could *blind* the camera."

"What does that mean?" Kathy asked.

"Tape it over," her brother replied. "The camera and light are on a wooden pole. I could sneak up behind them, in which case I'd be out of the camera's range. If I wore spiked boots, I'd go straight up the pole and tape over the camera lens." He sat up, grinning.

"Brilliant," Tom said, slapping him on the back. "We'll wait until the ranch lights are out, then grab a couple bags of garbage. If those guys are sleeping, they won't be checking the front entrance *or* the security camera. My guess is they're not too concerned about someone raiding their garbage."

"Wait a minute," Suzanne said. "You're forgetting something else. What if the camera isn't just giving a live feed, but recording? If those guys look over the previous night's footage each day, we'd have tipped them off—at the least."

"My bet is that if we don't alert them," Pete said, "they won't check the recording device. Chances are we can pull it off."

"One more hitch," Kathy said. "I'm sure Hank Pauley and his crew haul their wastepaper out to the dumpster every day. What happens if they realize some of their trash is missing? If they're doing something illegal, I bet they're darn careful about the trash. *Big problem.*"

"Ouch," Tom said. "How do we handle *that?*"

Suzanne had an idea. "Let's fill up a couple of those huge black garbage bags we have at home… with cardboard and paper stuff. We'll take them with us to exchange for the real thing. With luck, they won't spot the switch before the hauling company comes to empty it."

"Super," Tom said, his voice dropping into a conspiratorial whisper. "When do we do the dark, dire deed?"

After further discussion, they agreed that Monday night was the best bet. That would give them enough preparation time.

Kathy jumped up and cheered. "Awesome!"

The Chief walked into the living room, greeting the four home-grown detectives as he relaxed on the sofa. "I've got something for you. Remember the new guy who showed up at the ranch? A license plate check pulled up a gentleman named Richard Ulrich from Scottsdale. Guess where he works?"

Suzanne said, "Raydon Paper."

Her reply surprised the Chief. "How on earth did you guess that?" She related the phone call with Cooper Aviation.

"Well, that makes sense," he said. "Ulrich is an expert on printing security documents and financial instruments—bonds, banknotes, passports—things like that. It appears he works as a consultant."

A light went on in Pete's mind. "Oh, man. So they're doing something similar out at the ranch!"

"I think it's obvious, Pete," the Chief said. "They're running a printing operation of some kind. So what's your next move?"

"Well, we're going to check out their industrial garbage bin," Tom replied. "Figure out what's in there."

"Shredded wastepaper would be my guess," Suzanne said.

"Oh, good idea," the Chief said. "Remember, we don't know what's happening in that barn. It looks suspicious, I grant you that, but it might be a top-security project for a company, all aboveboard. Plus, the ranch is outside my jurisdiction. I could contact the sheriff, but if he pokes around out there, we might scare them off. Then they'd just set up shop elsewhere. We need more evidence first."

"Got it."

"So now there's Mike Lyons too," their father said. "Based on what Neil Vanderbilt witnessed over the past few weeks, I'd say we're dealing with human smuggling. Do you all see that?"

There was a murmur of assent.

"Here's the thing," he said, leaning forward. "I'm obligated to alert the federal authorities. Once I make that call, they'll be on his tail. If they arrest him, he might refuse to talk."

"In which case, we'll never find Angelina's mother," Kathy said.

"Exactly."

"What should we do now?" Suzanne asked, the corners of her

mouth turning down. "Our goal was to discover where Angelina came from, and we've done that. Now we need to locate her mother."

"Well, I understand, but we're in a tough spot," the Chief said. "The feds must be told. I can wait a day or two, but I'm obligated to alert them."

"Okay, thanks, Dad. We get it," Tom said.

"Watch yourselves," the Chief said. "Human smuggling is big business. It's likely that Mike Lyons and the people he's working with—or for—are dangerous."

11

ON THE MOVE

On Saturday, just after dinner, Suzanne's cell phone rang. "It's Neil Vanderbilt!" she yelled out to her brother. With Neil's number now added to her contacts, he was Unknown Caller no more.

"Hi, Neil," she said. "How are you?"

"Get out here. Something's happening." Then he disconnected. *Same as last time*, Suzanne thought.

"What does he want?" Tom asked as he raced into her room.

"He wants us out there," she said. "But he didn't say why. Neil is being his painful self."

Tom lit up on the run. "Let's go!"

On the way out, Suzanne called Kathy with the latest news.

"A man of few words," Kathy said. "Call me back if it's okay to join in. We don't want him clamming up with four of us appearing on his doorstep."

In June, sunset in Arizona occurred around 7:15 p.m. Dusk had settled as the twins pulled into the ranch. Neil was sitting on his porch, smoking a cigar, and eyeing his visitors. The dogs served as a welcoming committee.

"Meet Bart and Blackie." Tom grinned at the expression on Suzanne's face. "Believe it or not, they're friendly."

"So you've said." His sister recalled her first visit to the ranch. "I'll take your word for it."

"Thanks."

"You're welcome. Watch this."

Tom stepped out of the car and whistled. Both dogs tore over to him. He petted them while their tails thumped in the dust. Blackie rolled over on his back to have his tummy scratched.

Suzanne opened her door. The dogs rushed over and gave her a friendly welcome too. "Hi, Neil. I'm Suzanne. Remember me?"

"How could I forget?" he said. Suzanne eyed him carefully. *Tom and Kathy were right,* she thought. *He's different now, somehow.*

A minute later everyone was on the rooftop platform—including the dogs. Up top, a refreshing stiff breeze blew in their faces, bringing with it a pungent smell of summer grass. The telescope focused on the ranch belonging to Mike Lyons.

"Go ahead," Neil urged. "Check it out."

Suzanne peered into the viewfinder and adjusted the focus. On the circular front driveway, right behind the cargo truck, sat two late-model sedans.

Tom took her place and checked out the scene. "Neil, have you ever seen those vehicles before?"

"Nope. They followed each other in about an hour ago. The rancher greeted them, but the two new guys gave him a bad time."

"Any idea why?" Tom asked.

"Angelina, I imagine," he replied, irritated that Tom didn't get it. "The four of them retraced her steps, along the path she must have taken, walking from the barn out to the highway. They appeared to be ticked with Lyons. My guess is that he works for them, and they don't want to repeat the episode."

Suzanne received a message from Kathy. *Yes or no?*

No, fill you in later, she replied.

Tom peered through the viewfinder. "I can see one of the license plates. It's AZ M34597. Too dark for the other."

Suzanne recorded it. "Anything else new over there?" she asked.

"Nope. If there was, I'd have called you," Neil replied, turning around and heading down the stairs. Suzanne trailed him as the dogs raced ahead.

Tom glimpsed through the viewfinder one last time. As he did, the double garage door swung open. Fluorescent light cast a pale bluish glow into the gloom, illuminating a small group of people with suitcases. They walked single file toward the cargo truck.

"Hey, look!" Tom shouted.

Suzanne and Neil flipped around and rushed back onto the platform. The trio watched as five adults piled into the back of the truck.

"I'll be darned," Neil said. "Where did they come from?"

Mike Lyons stepped out of the house and slammed the truck's rear door shut.

"They're leaving," Tom said, jumping up and heading for the stairs. "Let's see where he takes them."

"Be careful," Neil advised. "These guys could be dangerous."

"Our father agrees with that," Suzanne replied.

Neil chuckled. "Always listen to Dad. What does your father do?"

"He's the chief of police for Prescott," Tom replied. The rancher's face dropped, noticeably.

The twins followed him to the bottom of the stairs, circling around to the front of the house.

"Much appreciated," Suzanne said. She was looking at Neil in a whole new light.

Tom shook his hand. "Thank you."

"Let's keep this to ourselves," Neil replied. "I don't want strangers rambling out here."

Tom glanced at his sister. "You bet."

The twins jumped into their car and headed out to Apache Canyon Drive.

"He didn't like it that Dad is the chief of police," Suzanne said.

"No fooling," her brother replied. "Let's park at the restaurant on 89. We can pick up Mike Lyons's truck at the intersection,"

Suzanne reached for her cell phone.

Kathy answered on the first ring. "Let us know which way they turn. Pete and I are heading out."

"I'll message you," Suzanne said.

Tom crossed the highway and positioned the Chevy in the parking lot, facing Apache Canyon Drive. They didn't have long to wait.

"Here he comes," Tom said. The large delivery truck came to the stop sign, its brakes squealing. Then it turned right.

Cargo truck heading into Prescott, Suzanne texted.

Kathy replied, *Got it.*

Tom let him gain a block before turning onto the highway. Soon four cars separated the two vehicles.

Passing Pleasant Creek Lane, Suzanne messaged.

We'll pick up on the interchange at Willow Creek Road, Kathy answered. Minutes later, Tom spotted the Brunellis, three vehicles behind Mike Lyons.

"Okay," Tom proposed. "Let them track him. Less chance of us being seen."

Take over, Suzanne typed. *Send updates, catch up in a few.* Tom dropped back a quarter mile.

Soon Kathy messaged, *Bus depot.*

"That makes sense," Tom said.

A minute later: *Four people with suitcases going into depot.*

"Why four?" Suzanne wondered out loud. "Where's the other one?"

Just as Tom pulled up, a lone adult female jumped from the truck's cargo space. Each of the travelers carried a suitcase.

Mike Lyons climbed back into the truck but didn't budge.

"I bet he doesn't move an inch until the bus pulls out," Kathy said.

"We've got to find out where they're going," Suzanne said. "I'll wander in there first."

Her brother hesitated for a moment. "You're right. Just be careful."

"No problem."

"There will be if you mess up."

Her anger flared for a brief second. "Speak for yourself, hotshot."

Suzanne stepped out of the car. The cargo truck had parked a little further up the road. Passing by, she glanced over at Mike Lyons, trying her best not to be obvious. He was busy looking down at his cell phone.

The depot doors opened, releasing a blast of frigid air. Suzanne walked into a giant, noisy waiting area. Children screamed, their cries bouncing off lofty ceilings. A stale-food odor permeated the atmosphere. Seats were at a premium.

She spotted the PURCHASE TICKETS window. Three departing buses were on the board, all leaving within the hour: Los Angeles, Chicago via Denver, and Phoenix.

It was easy to spot the five travelers. Each of them had one suitcase parked on the floor. They weren't sitting beside each other. Instead, they had spaced themselves at intervals around the depot.

One traveler had a boarding pass sticking straight up from his shirt pocket. Suzanne strolled over and sat across from him. He stood up and moved to another seat. *Someone coached him well.*

Suzanne grabbed a magazine and found a spot close to the lone woman.

"All aboard for Los Angeles, gate four!" blared over the loudspeakers. A couple dozen people stood, gathered their belongings, and walked out to a bus. The five travelers didn't move.

Suzanne glanced at the woman. She had no visible boarding pass and refused to make eye contact, even when Suzanne smiled at her in a friendly way. Nothing to do but wait for the next departure.

Soon the boys strolled in, one behind the other with only moments between them. Pete roamed around until he found an empty seat. Tom bought a magazine and buried his face in it. No one paid the slightest attention to them.

People continued to come and go. The level of noise increased as another departure loomed. Still, time dragged by in slow motion.

Meanwhile, Kathy sat in her car with an eye on Mike Lyons, feeling left out and bored to tears.

Later, another announcement blared over the loudspeakers. "All aboard for Phoenix, gate six!"

The five travelers rose, almost in unison, and joined a dozen other people passing through the depot's rear doors. Tom sauntered out to the car, followed by Pete. Mike Lyons still hadn't moved.

Suzanne checked the outside departure lane to be sure that the travelers had all boarded. They had, and within minutes the bus backed out, its horn blasting loud enough to wake the dead, and headed for Phoenix. She hiked out front just in time to see the cargo truck disappearing into the night.

The four friends had a quick conference in the Brunellis' car.

"Well, what now?" Kathy asked

"Someone has to meet that bus in Phoenix," Pete said, his eyes blazing with excitement. They were on to something—big too—and they knew it.

Suzanne couldn't agree more. "Those workers might lead us straight to Angelina's mother. I'm all for it."

"Who's going?" Tom asked. "It'll be a long night."

Pete groaned with disappointment. "We're helping Dad tomorrow morning. You're on your own."

12

SAFE HOUSE

The twins raced home to grab food and water for the trip to Phoenix. It promised to be a *very* late night.

The Chief encouraged his homegrown investigators. "Just be careful," he said, tossing a handful of healthy granola bars into their backpack. "Whatever you do, don't follow too close. If you lose them, there's always another day."

Sherri was out for the evening. "Otherwise we'd have a serious battle on our hands," Suzanne said aside to her brother. The twins knew their mother was, well, *cautious.*

With Tom at the wheel, they beelined to Interstate 10 and headed south to Phoenix. The on-line bus schedule showed one stop on the way to the city. There was little danger of missing its final destination. The hour-and-a-half trip was quiet and uneventful, and the late-evening traffic was light.

"I'm wired," Tom murmured, without even realizing he had said it out loud. They were both running on the energy of nervous anticipation.

"Good thing," his sister replied, laughing. "You're the one driving. I'll relieve you at midnight."

Later, as Suzanne looked out the window into the dark night, something occurred to her. "Angelina's mother must have traveled the same route. She would have passed by here a couple weeks ago."

"Maybe."

"No maybe about it."

Not long after, Tom passed a Greyhound bus. Suzanne caught the driver's gaze in the side mirror. "That's our guy," she said.

While Tom drove, Suzanne used her mapping app to locate the bus depot. She also messaged Kathy: *Just crossed into PHX city limits.* It was eleven o'clock. Traffic had picked up.

The twins parked close to the depot. They found an outside bench with a decent view of the arrival lanes. One bus was busy loading passengers. Minutes later, a second one pulled in—just a few lanes away—and came to a noisy stop. Sure enough, the five migrant workers disembarked and headed toward the street.

"Let's go," Tom said.

A van was waiting. The travelers piled in, and the vehicle zipped away from the curb. Tom followed, as far back as he could, without losing the vehicle in the sparse nighttime traffic. The last thing they wanted was to tip off the driver.

They headed west on Van Buren Street for a short distance, then north on a side street, until the van came to a sudden stop.

"Uh-oh," Tom said. "I think he's on to us." He drove past the vehicle without even a glance at the driver. Suzanne watched out of the corners of her eyes.

"You're right. They gave us the once-over as we passed by," she said.

Tom turned at the next intersection and circled the block. The twins lucked out—they spotted the van's brake lights in the driveway of a house that had seen far better days. There was just enough illumination cast by an adjacent overhead lamp to read the street number. The truck's passengers were hurrying inside as the Chevy passed.

"Bingo," Tom said. "That's where they're staying. The place is a wreck."

"Got it," Suzanne said in a hushed voice. She messaged the address to her father.

Tom pumped his arm up and down, elated. "Okay, let's head home."

It was long after 1:00 a.m. when they pulled into their driveway.

On Sunday morning, the Jackson and Brunelli families attended St. Francis Church. Later they enjoyed lunch at a local restaurant. Arizona is famous for its Mexican food, and they had discovered an authentic new eatery with spicy hot tamales and delicious cheese enchiladas—Pete's favorite.

"*Mmm-mmm,*" he said.

Suzanne nodded between bites. "Pass the hot sauce."

"And the water," Tom said, grasping his throat.

"Milk works better," Kathy reminded him.

On Sunday afternoon, at five o'clock sharp, the foursome met at the Jacksons'. Angelina played on the floor, dressing a doll that had belonged to Suzanne in her childhood.

"It was, like, wow," Suzanne said, describing the long trip. "The driver of the van tried to shake us, but we got lucky."

"We did," Tom said, his brow knit in thought, "but we don't have a clue what happened after they disappeared into that house."

"What do you mean?" Pete asked.

Sherri popped her head into the room. "Anyone need water?"

A chorus of "No, thanks!" rang out.

"Well," Suzanne replied, "do they stay in this house for only a day or two, then move to another location?"

"Or," Tom asked, "is Phoenix their last stop? Are they on the way to somewhere else, like California, for example? A lot of human traffickers are bringing migrant laborers north to work in agriculture—the golden state is a big destination for that."

"I get it," Kathy said. "But trafficked migrants often work in manufacturing too. If that's what's happening to Angelina's mom and her friends, where might that be?"

"We have to get back there," Tom said, "and see where they go next."

"If they're not already gone," his sister added.

A few minutes later, the Chief arrived home. He changed out of his uniform and joined the group in the family room. "Hi, everyone, how are things going?" He looked at his twins and grinned. "Did you catch some sleep?"

"Yeah, we're good," Tom replied. "Suzie's a little grumpy."

"Not," she retorted.

"Well, I have some interesting news for you," the Chief said. He sat down on the sofa. Angelina jumped off the floor and into his lap, wrapping her arms around his neck. "You know the address you sent me at midnight?"

"Yes." Suzanne sat straight up.

"Phoenix City Police said they're familiar with it," the Chief said. "It's a safe house for undocumented workers. People come and go. They'll stay for a few weeks, then leave after finding permanent work."

"How are the police handling it?" Pete asked.

"They don't, it's a waste of time," the Chief explained. "Whoever's running the place would just move to another location. Besides, the police focus on the human smugglers, not their accomplices." He paused for a few seconds. "Like Mike Lyons, for example."

"What kind of work would the women do?" Kathy asked.

"I asked the same question," the Chief replied. Angelina jumped on his knee. "Phoenix police told me that the men work in construction or agriculture as laborers, or as gardeners, groundskeepers, in pool maintenance—that sort of thing. The women often find work as seamstresses in the garment industry. They're paid next to nothing, because the sweatshop owners know the workers are undocumented. They come because they're desperate to find work, or to escape danger back home, but they can end up in situations far worse than they expect. Sometimes they're badly abused—especially the women. You can imagine."

In the silence that followed, Angelina—without even realizing it —became the center of everyone's attention. Suzanne pictured the child's poor mother, underpaid and overworked, almost like a slave, living in rotten housing, missing her daughter the whole time.

The Chief searched their faces. "Did you say one traveler was a female?"

"Yes," Suzanne replied.

"Okay. In that case, what should you do?"

Pete spoke up first. "Figure out where she works."

"Exactly," the Chief said. "That's what I'd do. Wherever that is, this little girl's mother shouldn't be far away."

13

DANGEROUS DIGS

Monday arrived, one week after a little girl had stumbled onto Highway 89.

After chores and lunch, the team gathered at the Jacksons' house and prepared two extra-large garbage bags, packed until they bulged with torn, shredded paper and cardboard. The finished bags, though lighter for sure than the ones they might replace, were plenty bulky.

"These would fool anybody," Pete said.

"Unless they open them up," his sister chided.

Soon they had stuffed the garbage bags into the Chevy's backseat and trunk. Then they taped over all the car's interior lights. Seen from the ranch house—or by the intrusive security camera—any glow could reveal their presence.

By late afternoon, it was just a matter of waiting.

All four had specific roles. While Tom and Pete raided the huge garbage bin, Kathy's job was to monitor the entrance to Apache Canyon Drive as she hid in the parking lot across Highway 89. If a car turned onto the road, she would warn them on an open phone connection.

Meanwhile, Suzanne would stand by the boys, ready to help, her eyes glued on the house. If there was movement from the ranch—even a hint—she would sound an immediate warning.

Everyone was in place by nine thirty. Kathy sat behind the wheel in her mother's car, with a view across the highway. She watched Suzanne and the boys turn onto Apache Canyon Drive and disappear into the darkness.

The only signs that anyone was home were the lights burning in the main house, the van parked out front, and a single vehicle in the open garage. The barn, closed and dark, gave away nothing. As the Chevy cruised past the ranch entrance, the camera didn't budge.

Suzanne and the boys hid in the deserted homesite across from Parker Hall's ranch, the same location where the drone had begun its epic flight a week earlier. From the secure hideaway, it was easy to see when things shut down for the night.

Around ten thirty, lights clicked off one after another. By eleven o'clock, the ranch house went dark.

"Okay, I'm going for it," Pete said. He carried a set of climbing boots with sharp spikes borrowed earlier in the day from a neighbor. "Wait for my signal. I'll point the flashlight at you from the top of the pole. Three flashes and you'll know we're ready to roll."

Pete slid out of the car and hurried over to the main road. Then he detoured into the ditch on the far side, disappearing into the dark. The idea was to sneak up *behind* the camera, well out of its range of vision.

The pole climb was much harder than he imagined. Along the way, he picked up a nasty splinter and his knees ached from the pressure of hanging on and pushing up at the same time. Even worse was balancing while he taped the lens—once he plunged down a few feet, barely saving himself from an absolute freefall. *That* little escapade sent his adrenalin racing.

Finally, he attached a long string to the masking tape and watched as the spool twirled down to ground level. One yank and the tape would free itself—no evidence left behind and no shimmying up the pole again.

Ten minutes later, a flashlight blinked three times from high above the entranceway. "There it is!" Tom shouted.

Suzanne pulled out of the homestead, headlights extinguished, turned onto Apache Canyon Drive, and coasted up to the ranch. Pete leaned against the bin like a triumphant warrior. He tossed the spiked boots into the back seat without saying a word.

Suzanne cut the ignition and slid out of the car. She left the driver's side door open before crossing over to the fence. She climbed up it, bending over the top, her eyes glued on the house. "Quiet as a mouse out here," she whispered. Next, she called Kathy. "We're parked in front."

Kathy cheered in a quiet voice: "Hooray! The adventure begins." The girls left their phones on with a live connection—just in case.

Pete pried up the steel lid of the industrial garbage bin. "Whoa, this thing is heavy." Tom darted over to help.

The stench of fresh printer's ink was overpowering. A quick burst of the flashlight showed that the bin was three-quarters full of huge black garbage bags—luckily, they were almost identical to the ones they had filled at the Jacksons'. Pete reached in and grabbed one, trying to yank it to the top. "*Way* too heavy."

"Just take what you can," Tom whispered in a hoarse voice. He helped drag a bag up to the edge of the bin. It wobbled for a few seconds before Tom gave it a hard pull, sending the bag crashing it onto the ground below him.

Suzanne jumped a foot. *"What are you guys doing?"* she hissed.

They looked around with apprehension. The loud thud had felt like an earthquake. But the camera remained motionless, the ranch dark. No one appeared to notice.

Except Kathy, listening on her cell phone. "What was *that?*"

"Not to worry," Suzanne whispered again. "Hotshot dropped a bag of garbage on the ground."

The boys wrestled the bag into the Chevy.

"Let's get one more and call it a night," Tom said.

"I'll jump inside the bin," Pete said. "There's gotta be a lighter one."

"Wait a sec," Tom objected. *Too late.* Pete sprang up, pulled himself over the edge and dropped down, shoving heavy bags around with his feet while bracing himself against a side wall. He dug his way to the bottom, touching the cold floor with his bare hands while bearing the weight of the bags above.

"Incoming car, incoming car!" Kathy's voice rang out in alarm.

As Suzanne sprinted over to the bin, Tom twisted toward the danger. "Pete, there's a car on its way in. *Get out of there!"*

"I can't! I'm in too deep," Pete cried out in a muffled voice.

Tom thought fast. "Okay! Don't worry. We'll throw our two bags on top."

They grabbed the decoy bags and tossed them in the dumpster. *"Stay down!"*

The twins leaped into the Chevy with Tom behind the wheel. He raced off to the hideaway, headlights still in the off position. Slowing for the homesite's grassy road, he executed a sharp turn to avoid revealing their presence with the car's brake lights. Suzanne gripped the edge of the dashboard as her body hit the side door. Tom cranked the car around to face the ranch and slammed the brakes hard, grinding to a stop.

That's when he remembered: "The lid to the garbage bin. *We left it open!"*

Panic seized Kathy as she listened in through Suzanne's phone.

A minute later, a sedan pulled up beside the ranch's front gate. Pete, his heart thumping hard, flattened himself along the cold floor, cheek to cool metal. *I'm screwed.* He could hear every word spoken.

"What the—who left the bin open?"

Pete heard two men getting out of their vehicle.

"Not me."

"Well, whoever did was very careless. We can't afford mistakes like this."

Someone uttered a bad word. "Is it full?"

"Yup. There's a ton of paper here."

"No harm done."

"Yeah, but Hank won't like it."

Bang! Pete's body jumped a foot. Someone had dropped the steel lid, allowing gravity to slam it shut. The electric gate opened, and the car drove off toward the ranch. The gate shut and locked with a loud *click*.

Silence enveloped the tight enclosure. Pete's heart slowed, working its way back to normal. It was over, he thought, but a horrible feeling overcame him. His throat tightened. It became harder to breathe. The walls seemed ever closer. He wanted out—*now*.

"Leaving the bin lid open wasn't too bright," Tom admitted to his sister, his voice subdued. "Still, it looks as if the fake bags saved us."

"Maybe not yet. *Look!*" Suzanne said, seeing ghostly figures moving on the ranch, their silhouettes revealed by a bobbing flashlight. She caught her breath. "They're coming back!"

"Whatever for?" Kathy gasped, her voice trembling.

Pete heard angry voices approaching, getting closer with every passing second. He couldn't burrow any deeper. *Okay, this is it. I've had it.* Three or four men were in a heated discussion. Words flew. The gate clicked open.

"I tell you, I closed that garbage bin."

"Well, it didn't open itself."

"Look, Hank, if I didn't close it, I'd know it."

The bin's metal lid swung up and open. A bluish glow from an LED flashlight flooded the interior. Someone punched a steel rod down into the garbage. The rod made it past the bags, deep into the bin, slamming onto the floor with a loud metallic thud. A second thrust, buffered by a solid bag of paper, stopped right above Pete's head—to his relief. A man grunted with the failed effort.

The final pass snagged Pete's jeans, pinching hard against his thigh before jolting to a stop. A wave of pain welled up, but Pete clamped his mouth shut with one hand. His mind spun. *My life depends upon it!* His body shuddered. Goosebumps raced up and down his spine.

"There's nothing unusual here," a voice said.

"Okay, but let's be more careful. Imagine if this stuff fell into the wrong hands."

"It's only shredded paper."

"Don't argue with me! Make sure this doesn't happen again."

Bang! The bin lid slammed shut once more. The voices walked away, still grumbling among themselves, and the gate closed. Pete hadn't moved a muscle, even though his leg ached with a burning pain. He exhaled into the paper, breathing through his mouth so he wouldn't gag on the pungent, inky odor.

The twins watched as the men ambled back toward the house, disappearing into darkness. This time it really was over. Relief flooded over Kathy as she listened to a tense play-by-play.

"Let's hope he's okay," Tom said over Suzanne's cell phone. "They're gone. I don't think we should risk trying to rescue him just yet."

Kathy and the twins waited in utter silence as minutes crawled by, but Pete couldn't stand another second. The walls seemed to close in, ever tighter, smothering him. He dug his way up, stood and raised the steel lid an inch, peeking out into the night, gulping down welcome draughts of cool air. There wasn't a soul anywhere. He gazed up at the camera—still motionless and non-threatening. The overhead light threw off its sickly yellow glow, but the ranch itself was dark.

Pete forced the lid open and squeezed his way out, gently lowering it behind him. Then he glided over to the wooden pole and grabbed hold of the string that dangled in a breeze. He yanked it hard, releasing the patch of tape that had covered the camera lens. The tape fluttered down, right into Pete's waiting hands. *Yes!* He eased himself into the ditch—out of range of the security camera—and limped back to the homesite. Soon he spotted the Chevy, hidden behind the trees.

The twins jumped a foot when their friend popped up in front of the car. "You scared us to death!" Suzanne exclaimed, one hand over her heart.

"Sorry," Pete said. "That garbage bin was driving me crazy. Hello, Kathy."

His sister squealed over the cell phone. "Pete, you creeped me right out!"

"It was worth it," he replied. Despite the pain, a big grin crossed his face.

"Sweet," Tom shouted. "Let's go see what we found."

SOON ENOUGH, TWO IMMENSE, HEAVY BAGS OF PAPER GARBAGE LANDED with thuds on the Jacksons' garage floor. The overpowering smell of ink wafted from the car and into the garage, engulfing them all.

"Well, we guessed right," Tom said. "A couple hundred pounds of shredded printed paper."

It turned out that Pete's leg was bleeding. It took him five minutes to wash and bandage his wound. "Looks worse than it feels," he told the others gamely.

They opened the bags, one at a time, and spread thousands of spaghetti-like strands of paper across the floor. When they finished the first bag, they swept up the mess and started again.

Later, the twins' parents returned home from a late dinner party. Sherri walked through the garage holding her nose. "What *is* that awful odor?" she complained.

"Did you find anything?" the Chief asked. They hadn't. He hung around for a few minutes, dipping his hands into the shredded paper with his homegrown investigators before heading off to bed.

It was laborious work.

"What *was* this stuff before they shredded it?" Tom wondered out loud.

"A gigantic headache," Kathy quipped, popping an aspirin. "Notice that it's laminated paper, thick too."

"Search me," Pete said. "Whatever it was, they didn't want it to see daylight."

It took about an hour to open each bag, dump out its contents, root through them, then re-bag and trash them.

By one o'clock in the morning, as they sifted through the last strands of paper, their hopes had flagged.

"Nothing," Suzanne said. "Just spaghetti."

That's when Kathy leaped to her feet, holding one thin strip of paper high in the air and shouting. "Eureka!"

14

TECHNOLOGY TO THE RESCUE

E lated, Kathy circled the garage in celebration.

"What'd you find?" Pete asked. He reached up and snatched the scrap from his sister.

"Manners," she protested, poking him in the side. Every so often her brother did something that seriously annoyed her.

The four mystery searchers gathered around to examine the three-inch long sliver of plasticized paper in Pete's hand.

Tom said, "Looks like it came from a passport page."

Suzanne shook her head. "No way."

"Way."

"Not," she argued.

Pete asked her, "Okay, so what is it?"

"The top part of a driver's license, of course."

"What makes you think so?" Tom said.

Suzanne's purse was sitting on a shelf in the garage. She dug around for a few seconds before producing her own driver's license. On the top—printed side-by-side—were the words:

ARIZONA DRIVER LICENSE USA

Suzanne lined the spaghetti strip against her license. "Perfect fit," she added said, mocking her brother with a sly grin.

"How amazing is that!" Kathy shouted, still excited with her discovery. She pumped one arm in the air. "You can see the top part of all four words,"

Tom surrendered. "Okay, you're right. You know what this means?"

"I do," Pete said, jumping in to point out the obvious. "They're printing phony IDs—for domestic use, not for international travel. Driver's licenses, not passports."

"Point made," Suzanne said. *"Exactly what undocumented workers need."*

A sudden feeling of euphoria washed over them. Their dangerous foray into Hank Pauley's world had proven its worth. And his nebulous connection to Mike Lyons—and, therefore, to Angelina and her mother—was now a fact.

One tiny, three-inch strip of plasticized paper was all it had taken.

ON TUESDAY MORNING THE TWINS PRESENTED THE LATEST EVIDENCE to their father. Their parents were finishing breakfast, but Angelina had yet to appear.

"She's a sleepyhead," Sherri said.

The Chief examined the thin three-inch strip and listened closely, asking questions. He poured himself another coffee, careful not to spill on his spotless uniform.

"Okay. Things have changed, for sure. It's obvious those guys are running an illegal printing operation out there. No one can legally print state driver's licenses except the state, obviously. Remember the plate number you recorded at Mike Lyons's place? Well, it turns out the car was a rental. He picked it up earlier at the airport. His driver's license was a phony—ditto for his credit card. He paid in cash before they ran it, so there's no way to track him. Law-abiding people don't carry false identification and bogus credit cards." He chuckled. "At least we know where the phony license came from."

"Here we go again," Sherri said. Alarm had crept into her voice. She looked at her twins. "A *lot* of bad guys are running around in this case."

"Not to worry," Tom assured their mother.

"We're always careful," Suzanne said.

"Very!" said Tom.

"One thing," the Chief added before leaving for work. "This tiny piece of plastic paper isn't enough evidence. You need more."

The twins glanced at each other, their eyes dancing.

"We haven't been chasing ghosts," Tom said.

"It makes the mystery worthwhile, doesn't it?" his sister replied.

THE FOURSOME GATHERED LATER THE SAME DAY AT THE BRUNELLIS'. The twins brought their friends up to date on Hank Pauley's unidentified visitor.

"Whoa!" Pete said. "So that guy had a phony driver's license. And his buddies are printing them. No shadow of a doubt, right? We're chasing real crooks."

Tom said, "Connected crooks too."

"What now?" Kathy asked.

Suzanne said, "We need to prove it."

Pete agreed. "Sure. Easier said than done."

"True. I've been mulling over an idea," Tom said, generating smiles from the group.

"Your ideas are dangerous," Kathy kidded him. "Tell us!"

"The action takes place in the barn, right? Remember the night we deployed the drone? That's when we spotted the monitors."

"I know where you're going," Suzanne perked up, looking at her brother.

"The problem," Tom continued, "is that the barn door is usually closed. But it opens every so often. If we got lucky—"

"—we might capture a shot of those screens," Suzanne completed his sentence.

"Here's the idea," Tom said, leaning closer. "We could install a hidden high-speed camera off their property. I can attach a powerful telephoto lens and point it straight at the barn."

Pete exclaimed, "Sneaky and devious too. I like it!"

Tom paused, thinking out the steps. "We can program it to capture an image every couple of minutes. If the camera ever catches the door open, we'll see *something*. Those screens are toward the back of the barn, but the camera will autofocus on the bright areas. We should be able to grab a tight close-up image." His enthusiasm was contagious.

"Not risky, either," Kathy said.

"Unless they catch you," Pete said.

Suzanne liked the idea. "Does the technology club have everything we need?"

"I think so," Tom said. "Best of all, the pictures transfer to us in a digital data dump. We can program the interval. Every few hours, for example. Or once a day."

Pete rubbed his hands together in glee. "Spy stuff. Even better."

"How difficult is it to hide the camera?" Kathy asked.

"It doesn't take much space. There's a grove of trees across the road, opposite the gate," Tom recalled. "We'll scout out the area, but it should work. All in favor?"

No one disagreed. When it came to technology, Tom was the acknowledged leader.

"Okay."

"Let's do it."

"Nice. Can you imagine those images rolling in every few hours?"

Tom reveled in their enthusiasm. "First, we need permission from Ray. I doubt whether that will be a problem."

They discussed the intricacies of the idea for the better part of an hour. Tom planned on allowing three hours to test the software and hardware and program the unit. The meeting ended.

On the way home, Suzanne lapsed into silence.

"Earth to Suzanne," her brother pinged. "What's up?"

"Oh, I was just thinking about Hank Pauley. That man is dangerous," Suzanne thought out loud. "He'll do whatever it takes to protect his operation. Are we sure we should do this?"

"Darn sure," Tom replied. "No mistakes. Not even one."

ON WEDNESDAY MORNING, THE TWINS CRUISED OUT TO SEE RAY Huntley. Tom asked to borrow the camera system—for a week.

"No problem," Ray assured his visitors. "But the telephoto lens is in rough shape. Somebody dropped it..."

"Okay, thanks. I'll rent one from Joey's Camera," Tom said.

"How goes the hunt for Angelina's mother?" Ray asked.

Suzanne shot him a thumbs-up. "It's promising."

On the trip home Tom turned right onto Apache Canyon Drive. They drove past Parker Hall's ranch, checking out a viable camera location.

"Hey, look!" Suzanne exclaimed, sitting up with a startled expression. "Isn't that Mike Lyons's truck?" Two men stood in front of the closed barn.

"For sure. And he's standing there, talking with Hank Pauley. Read the body language. Those two guys are friends."

"Partners, more likely."

"I'd bet on it," Tom said. "Still, we really don't know anything, including how often that door opens. Nor what days they work. We can only hope we get a lucky shot or two."

He drove another few hundred yards before u-turning the Chevy. As they passed the trees across from the gate to the ranch, Suzanne grabbed a few shots. A viable camera location wouldn't be a problem.

"Easy to hide too," Tom said. "Check out all those leaves."

BY LATE AFTERNOON THEY HAD THE CAMERA PROGRAMMED AND READY to go. The Brunellis stopped by to help. Together, the four friends positioned the hardware in the Jacksons' backyard with the telephoto lens focused on a parked vehicle a block away. Every two minutes the camera auto-captured a new shot. Half an hour later a digital dump of fifteen pictures landed on Tom's cell phone.

"Picture perfect, right on time," he noted with satisfaction. Cheers rang out. The photos were clean and sharp.

"This is just amazing," Pete said. "You can read the make and model of the vehicle."

"It'll work," Tom said. "The shots will come in like clockwork."

"When do we install it?" Kathy asked.

"Tonight," Tom grinned. "Why wait?"

15

PICTURE PERFECT

Brisk, cool mountain breezes swirled across a moonless night. The foursome returned to familiar territory having swallowed a large dose of apprehension. Taking on Hank Pauley wasn't anything they relished.

Suzanne drove the Chevy, cruising past the ranch just after 10:00 p.m. beneath the ghostly pale yellow of the overhead street-light out front. Lights were burning everywhere in the ranch house too, but not in the barn.

"It'll be a late night," Tom said.

The security camera's position appeared mobile through nearly 180 degrees side to side and up and down, suggesting that its coverage included the entire entrance area and many yards beyond in all directions. They eyed the intrusive device, but it didn't budge.

"No one's paying attention in the house," Pete said.

Tom replied, "Works for me."

Their first stop was the deserted homesite. As Suzanne turned in and the Chevy ground to a halt, Kathy jumped out, carrying a pair of powerful binoculars.

"Later."

"Have fun."

"Always." She slipped behind the trees.

Suzanne turned the car around and drove back, straight through the overhead cone of light. A hundred yards farther delivered them outside their estimated maximum possible range of vision of the security camera. The vehicle came to a complete stop.

"Go!" Pete urged.

Tom threw the backseat passenger door open and sprang out onto the gravel road. He grabbed the box of equipment, hopped over a fence, and disappeared into a gully. It took only seconds. Pete leaned over and shut the door. The Chevy raced off toward the highway.

They stayed in touch with an open phone line, using ear pods and mics.

"Everything okay, Tom?" Pete asked.

"Considering where I am, yeah. Over the fence, heading for the trees."

Suzanne found a parking place at the restaurant on 89, turning to face Apache Canyon Drive. "Good enough?"

"Perfect," Pete replied. Their job was to watch for an incoming vehicle or rescue the other two in an emergency.

"Kathy, are you on?" Suzanne asked.

"Reporting for duty, ma'am," she replied with a giggle. Kathy had located a comfortable spot behind a windbreak, offering a straight-line angled view of the ranch house. "All is quiet."

"You okay, Tom?" Pete asked.

"So far," he replied, his voice muffled.

With Tom's microphone live, the other three could hear his breath coming faster over time. Climbing trees, hauling equipment, and working at high speed were all taxing. He reported in often. "I've found the ideal location in the crook of a tree. It's about six or eight feet from ground level. I'll rip the foliage off for a clean visual path to the barn."

Five minutes later, the camera secure, Tom locked it in place with wire. "The green netting will hide it." The sound of breaking branches and leaves being torn away filled the open line. "Okay, I'm sending a test now."

At that moment, a dog barked.

"The front door of the ranch house *just opened,*" Kathy warned.

"Uh-oh," Tom blurted, his heart instinctively pumping faster. Under the yellow light he spotted a German shepherd, peering across the roadway, barking without stop.

"Watch out, Tom," Kathy's voice notched up in alarm. "Two men, coming your way. *Hide, quick!*"

Footsteps rushed out on the gravel.

Tom whispered in a hoarse voice. "There's a large dog out here— first time we've seen him. I'm going higher up the tree."

"Should we drive back?" Suzanne asked.

"No!"

A voice yelled, "What's up, you crazy dog?"

Eucalyptus trees can grow huge, and this one was at least sixty feet tall. Tom climbed, higher and faster, pulling up the now almost empty equipment box behind him. His breath soon came in gasps.

A second man shouted, "Let the dog free. What's he's after?"

The animal raced across the road, slipped through the fence, and paused under the eucalyptus tree. He looked straight up and circled the trunk, barking ferociously. Tom sat motionless, scrunched up, trying his best to be invisible.

A powerful beam of light projected up from ground level. It danced through the thick foliage, creating a moving kaleidoscope of rays and shadows. Tom buried himself deeply among the large green leaves. He could hear every word spoken.

"Stupid dog. I'll bet he's got a raccoon treed up there."

"As long as it's not a skunk or a bobcat, I don't care!"

Both men laughed. "C'mon dog, get out of there."

One of them grabbed the dog by the collar. It yelped. They crossed the road, driving the German shepherd before them. The barking stopped.

In the distance someone else shouted, "What is it?"

"He chased an animal up a tree!" the first voice hollered in response. Footsteps receded. There was more laughter. The voices faded.

"They're back in the house," Kathy reported, her eyes locked onto the scene in her binoculars. The front door closed.

Tom, his heart still pounding, replied, "Yeah, they're gone." He guessed that he had climbed thirty feet up or more.

"Whoa. That was close," Pete said.

"Definitely. But we passed the first test."

"Which was?" Suzanne asked.

"They pointed a flashlight straight up the tree but didn't spot the camera."

"Better yet, they didn't spot you," Kathy said.

"I've got good news," Suzanne said. "The image on my cell phone is perfect."

"Great," Tom replied. "Come get me." He let the nearly empty box fall to the ground and began the long climb down, one branch at a time.

Suzanne and Pete cruised out to the hidden homesite to pick up Kathy. Then they shot over to the pickup spot, past the ranch entrance, and stopped. The ranch was completely dark now and eerily quiet.

Somehow—at that exact moment—the beast had made it back to the gate. He began to bark his head off once more.

"I can't believe it," Tom muttered to himself.

Pete leaned over and flung the backseat passenger door open. Tom leaped out of the ditch and into the seat, tossing his equipment box in first. Suzanne tore off toward the highway.

Safely in the back of the Chevy, Tom and Kathy turned around, studying the security camera through the rear window.

"That camera's turning toward us!" Tom exclaimed.

"You bet it is," Kathy said. "The nasty thing is following us."

At the gate was an illuminated, receding form—a man, moving fast, pointing at their vehicle. The scene cut away as Suzanne executed a sharp curve toward 89.

Pete exhaled in relief. "That was close."

"Seriously close, but we made it!" Kathy whooped.

"Yahoo!" Suzanne shouted.

Tom stared into the ink-black night. A feeling of dread had overtaken him, nagging in his mind. *How strong a scent did I leave on that tree?* He didn't like the feeling. Not one bit.

ON THURSDAY MORNING, JUST AFTER TEN, NINETY stills downloaded on their cell phones. Tom had programmed the unit to begin recording at 7:00 a.m., capturing a still every two minutes. The camera sent digital dumps three hours apart, shifting into overnight hibernation mode after a twelve-hour run to conserve its battery.

The twins scanned each shot and called their best friends.

"Any thoughts?" Tom asked. "Anything strike you as interesting?"

"There are five men," Kathy said, "and that doesn't include Hank Pauley."

"We didn't catch the barn door open," Suzanne said. "They must've walked in and closed it immediately between shots."

"They start work early," Pete noticed. "They're at it by 7:00 a.m."

Kathy giggled. "The mystery deepens."

THE DIGITAL DUMPS CONTINUED LIKE CLOCKWORK, ALTHOUGH THE barn door remained closed—frustrating the foursome to no end—before they caught a break: just before its 7:00 p.m. shutdown on Thursday evening, the camera caught the barn door open for twenty minutes straight, yielding ten clean shots of the interior.

"A bonanza," Tom said as they clicked through the pictures Friday morning.

"We lucked out big time," Kathy said.

The camera captured images of the men hauling freight out

through the front door. It was obvious the helicopter had just returned.

"Finished product," Pete said. "I'd love to peek inside one of those boxes."

As expected, some indeterminable software application dominated the monitor screens. "I bet that they have a custom-designed app that runs the press automatically," Tom said, "while the hired help mainly does the physical labor."

In the foreground appeared sealed boxes, ready for shipping. By the next frame, the tenth, the door had closed again.

"It's exciting to see the stills come in, disappointing that we can't prove what they're doing out there," Kathy said, nailing the conundrum they now faced.

The last digital dump of the day transferred that evening. By then, the foursome's hope was dwindling.

The four friends, quiet and dispirited, met at the Brunellis' to scan through the final shots. Pete plugged his laptop into the large-screen monitor. They examined each still, finding most of them similar to hundreds of others—nothing but a closed barn door. But the thirty-second still in the sequence hit pay dirt.

Pete leaped into the air, pointing at the screen. "Can you believe it?" He threw his head back and laughed.

The barn door had opened long enough to capture a single revealing shot. Blowing up the image on one of the computer screens, they could make out a close-up scan of an uncut sheet of thirty-six drivers' licenses—in six even rows of six—for the State of California.

Tom enlarged the image. It was possible to read the name—and see the face—on each license. The camera was that good.

Suzanne was beside herself. "There's the proof! They're printing phony IDs, and not just for Arizona. I bet they're doing lots of other states too—maybe even the whole country."

"Just as we suspected, that's how Hank Pauley and Mike Lyons are connected," Tom said, raising one arm in the air. "Lyons needs the phony ID for his passengers."

Pete rubbed his hands together in glee. "What else is here?"

"We don't need more. We found what we're looking for," Kathy said, standing with both arms in the air.

"You never know," Tom replied. "Hit it, Pete."

Pete touched Next on his controller and continued to scroll through the images. The barn door closed once again. Everything was routine—until the final still appeared.

Suzanne drew back into the couch. "My gosh, it's *him!*"

There, with his huge head filling the screen, scowling into the camera, was the sinister, shocked face of Hank Pauley.

"Well, that's a little awkward," Kathy quipped.

"We're toast," Pete said. "They spotted the camera! How did that happen?"

"The dog must've tipped them off," Tom said, devastated. "They went back to look at the tree again. I knew it. That's what was worrying me. There goes our borrowed surveillance equipment."

Kathy shrank down into the sofa right beside her best friend. "Time to call for reinforcements."

16

CLOSING IN

"All four of us—in one car? Hiding in a strange neighborhood, at six in the morning? I don't think so," Kathy said.

Suzanne agreed. "For sure. That would draw far too much attention. Guys, you figure out what's going on, then we'll come and join you."

And so, early Friday morning, Tom parked the Chevy half a block from the house in Phoenix where the undocumented migrant workers had disappeared a few days before. It was a little after 6:00 a.m., almost broad daylight.

Pete yawned, stretching out, touching the ceiling behind the front seat. It had been a long drive and a boring wait. "I'm hungry. When do we eat?"

"I bet they start early," Tom replied, "soon for sure."

"Geez, I hope you're right."

Half an hour later, a van pulled into the driveway of the Phoenix home, as close to the door as possible. The boys' eyes glued to the scene as eight adult males hurried from the house. They climbed in and the vehicle zipped away from the curb, disappearing within seconds.

"We were right," Tom said. "Next up, I'm guessing, are the ladies."

Sure enough, the van returned minutes later. "Four, five, six..." Pete counted, as a group of young women found seats. The driver slammed the door shut.

"You think one of them is Angelina's mother?" Pete asked.

"Who knows?" Tom replied, firing up the car. "Let's go." Things were working out according to plan.

Morning rush-hour was heavy, but Tom found it easy to stay close. The Chevy blended in with the traffic.

"That driver's not taking any evasive action," Pete said. "This is what he does every day. It's routine."

Minutes later, the van pulled up to a huge old building in a dated-looking industrial park. The boys hung back as six women, carrying purses and lunch bags, stepped out of the vehicle and merged into a teeming crowd of workers. They soon vanished behind double glass doors.

High up on the building's façade was a large sign: RAMONA'S LEATHER WORKS.

"Okay, this is it," Tom said, elated with their success so far. The number of people making their way in soon dwindled to nothing. "Seven a.m. is the magic hour."

Pete said, "I'm starving. Let's grab a bite."

"Me too." Tom sped off, weaving his way back to Interstate 17, searching for the closest takeout food.

"I'd guess that Angelina's mother was in that van," Pete said.

"Good chance of that," Tom said, "and I'd bet she's in that building right now."

"How are we gonna rescue her?"

"Good question."

"HOW WILL WE GET HER *OUT*" KATHY ASKED, A FEW HOURS LATER, AS the foursome met in the Jacksons' living room.

"It won't be easy," Tom replied.

"But it's exciting, isn't it?" Suzanne said. "Angelina's mother can't be far away."

"There's only one way," Kathy said, looking at Suzanne. "You and I have to get inside that building."

"And do what, exactly?" her brother challenged.

"Exactly what we should," she fired back.

"You know what, Kathy? You're right," Suzanne said.

"I agree," Tom said.

Pete looked at his best friend in disbelief. "So they get in. *Then what?* No one's gonna be happy to see them."

"Angelina's mother will," Suzanne replied.

"You don't know that."

"You're being weird."

"Define weird."

"You, for example."

"Wait a minute," Tom jumped into the fray. "We *have* to get in there. There's no other option."

"*How?*" Pete asked. "That place is like a labor camp for undocumented workers. I'm sure whoever runs it keeps a sharp eye on the help."

"They couldn't all be undocumented," Suzanne said.

"Sure they could."

"I doubt it."

"Doesn't matter," Pete said. "Strangers won't be allowed in there. No way are you gonna drag away one of their workers."

"You're no help," Kathy chided her brother. He glared back at her.

Suzanne hesitated. "The worst thing they can do is throw us out. They won't have us arrested for trespassing—not if they're using undocumented labor. They wouldn't dare."

"You might be surprised," Pete argued.

Everyone lapsed into silence, mulling things over before Tom snapped his fingers. "I've got it. Pete, remember how just before 7:00 a.m., when there were dozens of women heading into work?"

"Sure," Pete recalled. "More than that. I bet there were two hundred. Or more."

"The girls can walk right through the doors. No one would pay the slightest attention to them in the middle of that crowd."

"Maybe. Then what?"

"Then we're in there," Kathy said, standing. "We can talk to people, show a picture of Angelina, ask if anyone knows her mother."

"Perfect," Suzanne said, her voice rising in excitement. "Love it. Better yet, we'll create a flyer and pass it out."

"The management will get to us," Kathy said, "but it'll be too late."

Pete gave in to the idea with a grudging sigh. "Okay. I like the flyer bit. They'll think you're union organizers or something—you won't be chatting with people, that's for sure. What if they try to hurt you?"

"Well, those are risks we have to take," said Suzanne. "For Angelina's sake."

"And her mom's," Kathy added. "When do we do it?"

"It's a slave camp," Pete said. "They'll be working tomorrow."

ON SATURDAY MORNING, THE FOUR YOUNG MYSTERY SEARCHERS parked a few doors south from Ramona's Leather Works. It was a few minutes before 7:00 a.m.

"Ready?" Tom asked.

"Darn right," Suzanne replied, taking a deep breath.

"Be careful," Pete said. "If something goes wrong, we'll be standing out front. Scream loud!"

"My hero," his sister said. For all her bravado, she felt nervous, even apprehensive.

Suzanne grasped a satchel with a couple hundred flyers inside. The handout featured a large close-up picture of Angelina, together with the following notice:

ANGELINA ESTÁ EN BUSCA DE SU FAMILIA.
¿ES USTED SU MADRE?
¡LLÁMEME POR FAVOR, LE PUEDO AYUDAR!

ANGELINA IS SEARCHING FOR HER FAMILY.
ARE YOU HER MOTHER?
PLEASE CALL ME, I CAN HELP!

SUZANNE'S NAME AND CELL PHONE NUMBER APPEARED BELOW.

"It's now or never."

The girls slipped out of the car into a large crowd of women, many chatting amiably in Spanish as they flowed along an old, broken sidewalk toward Ramona's Leather Works. Suzanne, the taller of the two, stood out with her fair skin and auburn-colored hair. Kathy, shorter and with olive skin and coal-black hair, melted into the throng. The boys watched them all the way to the double glass doors, propped open for easy access.

"It's 7:00 a.m. on the nose," Pete said. There wasn't a woman to be seen. The boys jumped out of the car and made their way to the front of the building, loitering on the steps outside, ready for anything.

Inside, as the morning's final burst of workers circled around him, a bored young man sitting at a large entry desk yawned. The women strolled through the swinging doors behind him, fanning out to individual workstations in a huge, windowless cavern.

Suzanne and Kathy glanced at each other. *We made it.*

The girls caught their breath at the swirl of activity—a chaotic, organized scene of rising dust, dirt, and smoke. A pungent smell of burned leather filled their lungs. Dozens of women were operating an assortment of sewing machines and cutters. The clacking noise was deafening.

The girls searched the floor, warily looking for whoever was in charge. But they couldn't identify a supervisor of any kind.

They locked eyes. "Walk side by side, pass them out," Suzanne mouthed. She handed Kathy a neat stack of half the flyers.

There were ten workstations in each row, with a couple dozen evenly spaced rows in total. The girls zigzagged down the lines in rapid motion, trying not to attract attention, dropping a handout off for every worker.

The operators were bent over, focused on their work. Every so often a seamstress glanced up to accept the flyer in her hand. The girls had covered more than half the stations before they noticed that the noise level had tapered off.

"Look," Suzanne mouthed, tapping Kathy on her shoulder. Many of the seamstresses had stopped working. They were pointing at the flyers and talking among themselves.

Just then, two large, imposing women appeared from nowhere, rushing over to the girls and screaming at them in Spanish.

Supervisors, Kathy realized. *"Look out!* Here they come."

"¿Qué haces aquí? ¡Vete!" they shouted.

"They want to know what we're doing here," Suzanne mouthed again. "They're throwing us out." The women pushed them forward, herding them back toward the swinging doors in quick, rude motions.

Suzanne and Kathy moved—there wasn't any other choice—but refused eye contact, ignoring the supervisors as they continued to drop flyers wherever they could.

"Stop that. Get out now!" one woman shouted in heavily-accented English, adding a swear word and shoving them once more. The huge cavern went deathly quiet, the machines grinding to a halt. Every eye was upon them.

Suzanne's temper flared, her face turned fire-engine red. *"Don't even think of us pushing us!"*

The girls reached the swinging doors and hustled through. At the front desk the young man sat straight up, open-mouthed and alert, watching the dramatic scene play out before him.

"Okay, okay, we're leaving," Suzanne said. She struggled to gain control again. "Bien, nos vamos." It was hard to argue with anyone that big.

"Don't come back again!" one of the huge women barked. She sliced a finger across her throat.

"Never!" added the other, ominously.

With one last shove, the girls stumbled out through the double front doors and into the fresh, welcome air. The sun was shining.

At the sight of the two boys, rising in opposition, the supervisors backed off and contented themselves with scowling at the four intruders from behind the glass.

"Mission accomplished," Suzanne said, her heart pumping fast, her eyes huge.

"It worked," Kathy gasped. "It really worked!"

17

ANGELINA'S MAMÁ

"Now what?" Suzanne asked.

"Now we wait to see if she approaches us after work," Tom said.

"You mean we park out front?" Pete asked.

"Sure, why not?" Kathy replied.

Pete shrugged. "Hey, I'm all for it."

"Me too," Suzanne said. "But I bet those two awful supervisors will guard the workers when they come out."

Pete grinned. "Told you, didn't I?"

"You're a regular genius," his sister quipped.

They spent the morning at the Phoenix Art Museum. Lunch at Hamburger Haven was great too. Much of the afternoon slipped away as they toured Arizona State University in nearby Tempe, one of the largest campuses in the nation.

Minutes before four o'clock, Tom pulled the Chevy up to Ramona's Leather Works, parking across the street from the double front doors. Tom guessed the workers would get off work no later than four thirty.

Pete agreed. "Not earlier."

"Kathy and I will stand out beside the car," Suzanne said. "They'll recognize us, I'm sure."

"Okay," Tom said. "We'll be ready to roll if she comes over."

The young man from the front desk propped open the doors. Seconds later, the two supervisors strode out and stood like sentinels—arms folded, threatening, and mean-looking.

"They spotted us," Kathy said. Sure enough, the supervisors glared in their direction. One of them made a crude gesture toward the girls.

"No one will approach us with those two creeps on guard," Suzanne said, disgusted.

At that moment, the familiar black van pulled up as the workers streamed out from the sweatshop. The vehicle loaded quickly and pulled away from the curb.

Was Angelina's mother on board?

The young man returned and closed the front doors, but the supervisors didn't budge an inch. Their eyes continually bored into the teens.

"Okay, we're wasting our time," Tom said, staring back at the obnoxious women. The girls jumped into the backseat. As the Chevy pulled away from the curb, there was a final rude gesture from one of the awful supervisors.

"Nice," Kathy said. "Just in case we didn't get the message first time around."

Pete said, "Can you say *creep?*"

"She's got my phone number," Suzanne said, a half smile on her face.

"Who does?" Kathy asked.

"Angelina's mother. She's got my phone number," Suzanne repeated.

"So does management at Ramona's Leather Works," Pete said.

Suzanne replied, "Who cares?" She tossed her head. "They don't worry me in the slightest."

THE TWINS DIDN'T RETURN HOME UNTIL LATE THAT NIGHT. THEIR
parents had turned in an hour earlier. Suzanne had fallen into a
deep sleep when her cell phone buzzed under her pillow. She
awoke, glancing at the screen. Area code 602. *Phoenix!*

"Hola! ¿Bueno? Soy Suzanne," she said, sitting up in bed. "Hello?
This is Suzanne."

There was a long pause. "Soy Teresa," a young woman's voice
replied.

Suzanne jumped up and raced into Tom's bedroom, shaking him
awake.

"Teresa, gracias por contactarme," she said. *Thank you for calling
me!* Suzanne thought. "¿Eres la madre de Angelina?" *Please say you're
her mother...*

"Sí, sí," Teresa said, sobbing.

"It's Angelina's mother!" Suzanne said, translating for her groggy
brother. "She wants to know if her daughter is safe."

Teresa was crying even harder now. "Sí, sí, en seguridad," said
Suzanne, "y viviendo aquí con mi familia." She turned to Tom again:
"I said, 'Safe and living here with us.'" Tom was almost fully awake
now. "Esta bien. Ella te echa de menos."

The twins' eyes locked. "I said, 'She's doing well, but she misses
you.'"

Teresa interrupted Suzanne in an urgent whisper.

"She says she can't talk," Suzanne said, "because they might catch
her—she's using a borrowed phone."

"Ask her how we can help get her out of there," Tom said.

After a short back and forth, Suzanne could offer only a discouraging answer. "The only time she's free is when she walks from the
van to the front doors of Ramona's in the morning—and back at
night."

"Could she run away then, at that moment?"

Suzanne conferred with an increasingly panicked-sounding
Teresa again. "She says the supervisors guard them all the time."

"What if we parked out front Monday morning?" Tom whispered. "And you or Kathy stand outside our car?"

Suzanne explained the idea to Teresa. "She says yes, she'd recognize us."

"Tell her we'll leave the back door open," Tom continued, closing his eyes and picturing the scene. "She can slip into our car on the way in. Then we'll take off."

Teresa hesitated for a long moment before agreeing. "Lo intentaré lo mejor que pueda. Gracias—" *Click.*

"She said she'd try her best," Suzanne said. Then she threw her phone down onto the bed. "Darn it."

"What's the matter?"

"She disconnected too fast. We *still* don't even know her last name!"

18

ONE CHANCE

In the car, speeding along the dark and empty highway to Phoenix on Monday morning, the foursome had plenty of time to argue over all the things that could go wrong with their rescue plan. Everyone realized that they had one shot—*and only one*—at rescuing Teresa.

"If we miss this, we're dead," Tom, at the wheel, said. He glanced at Pete, sitting beside him in the front passenger seat. "They'll make her disappear, and we'll never see her again."

A shiver ran up Suzanne's spine. "If we miss this, *she'll* be dead."

"Do you think they would hurt—?" Tom started.

Suzanne cut him off in mid-sentence. "I don't know."

"You're being awfully dramatic," Pete said.

"You're being terribly rude," his sister shot back at him. Kathy tried to reassure her friend. "Don't worry, Suzie, we'll save her," she said, without even a glance at her brother.

They decided there was no reason to return to the safe house in Phoenix. "Why risk alerting the driver of the van to our presence?" Kathy argued.

After an early breakfast at a city diner, they headed straight to

Ramona's Leather Works. Tom drove, threading the Chevy through
the early morning traffic, doing his best to ignore the bickering.

Soon, the factory appeared in front of them. The silence in the
car was absolute. Tom pulled a U-turn and parked, just in front of
the spot where they had seen the van park previously.

It was six forty. Knowing that both his parents were early risers,
Suzanne called home to let them know that the foursome had safely
arrived. Sherri answered just as she was walking into the kitchen to
fix her breakfast. They chatted for a minute when from nowhere
Sherri said, "Perez."

"Pardon me?" Suzanne asked.

"Angelina's last name. It's Perez."

She put her mother on speaker. "Where did you learn that?"

"Angelina told me at bedtime. She's found her voice again and is
talking up a storm. Something else too," their mother added.
"Angelina will turn five on her next birthday, but she's not sure
when."

"So her mother's full name is Teresa Perez," Kathy said.

Tom nodded his head. "You bet it is."

"Mom, we have to go," Suzanne said. She disconnected. Cars,
trucks and vans had appeared, each one dropping off a handful of
noisy, dark-haired women. Soon the Jacksons' car disappeared
behind a moving throng of workers that packed the sidewalk, all
heading toward the double glass doors.

"They're here!" Pete shouted.

The twins and Kathy twisted around in their seats to see the
black van as it slowed, its right signal light blinking red. It pulled to
the curb and came to a halt just behind the Chevy. *So far, so good,*
Suzanne thought. It was three minutes before 7:00 a.m.

The four friends hesitated a few seconds, trying to time it just
right. Kathy opened the car's back passenger door.

Pete broke the silence. "Don't move until you see someone get
out," he whispered. The van's side door slid open, and its first occu-
pant stepped onto the sidewalk *"Go!"* he urged. "Go, Kathy!"

"Watch out," Suzanne warned. "Those awful supervisors are out front." Sure enough, Kathy spotted them within seconds. They hadn't seen her—yet. Her short stature and coal-black hair made her all but invisible on the teeming sidewalk. Still, the car stood out as the only parked vehicle.

Kathy left the backdoor open, her hand on the door handle, standing tight against the side of the vehicle, trying to look casual.

A second, third and fourth woman dropped out of the van. Kathy's eyes darted back and forth between the van and the two nasty guards.

One of them pointed to the Chevy and mouthed something. They began striding over, hampered as they struggled against a tide of workers.

Those extra seconds were a lifesaver.

"Look out!" Pete hollered, warning his sister.

A small, panic-stricken woman, her arms tightly wrapped around a folded grocery bag, lunged toward Kathy. "Soy Teresa!" she cried.

"Get in, quick!" Kathy urged, giving her a solid push toward Suzanne, jumping in behind her, and slamming the door shut. Tom hit the lock button. *Click!* The supervisors reached the side passenger doors, their faces twisted in anger, grabbing at the handles. They hammered on the window. *"Give her back!"* one screamed in Spanish. The other one spit at the car. Their language turned fowl.

Too late! Tom hit the gas pedal, and the Chevy peeled away.

Teresa was sobbing, her face buried in her hands, her head hanging down. Silence descended on the cabin.

"Teresa," Suzanne said, softly. "You're safe. Estás a salvo." She translated for the Brunellis—their second language was Italian. "It's over. Está terminado."

Kathy said, "You'll be okay." She gave Teresa a big hug.

Suzanne took Teresa's hands in her own and held them tight, assuring the young woman that her daughter awaited. "Angelina te espera." That sent Teresa into a deluge of fresh tears.

Tom drove on, not saying a word. Pete was silent too. The boys listened to the drama unfolding in the backseat. The Chevy headed straight for Interstate 17 and home.

———

By lunchtime the group had made it back to Prescott. Tom had called ahead, arranging for Teresa to move in with her daughter and the Jackson family for a while.

When Teresa walked through the front door, Angelina leapt up and ran into her mother's arms screaming, "Mamá, mamá!" For the next hour she clung to her mom, refusing to let her go. Teresa cried once more, but joyous tears of reunion and happiness. Sherri took over, showing the little Perez family to their bedroom, with help from Angelina.

"We did it," Suzanne said, looking around at the group. They high-fived each other. *"We really did it!"*

"Don't forget Neil Vanderbilt," Kathy said. "He made it possible."

"Without him, we wouldn't have found Teresa," Tom said.

Suzanne called, but he refused to answer his cell phone.

"Same old guy." Pete said. "He'll never change."

———

Later, after things had settled down, Teresa's story came out, one piece at a time, as she sat holding her little girl in her lap. And, that same evening, after Teresa and Angelina had retired, the Brunelli and Jackson families met, talking late into the night. It had been two days since the twins had last caught up with the Chief. Although there was big news to share with him, everyone's focus was on Teresa.

"She's a single mom from Hermosillo, Mexico," Suzanne explained. "Her hope was a better life for herself and her daughter, but it was rough from the start. Before leaving Mexico, the human smugglers demanded more money. Either Teresa accepted their terms or lost what she had paid them. She agreed and plunged ahead."

"Then Mike Lyons picked her up," Kathy said, taking over the narrative. "It was his turn. He blackmailed the whole group, demanding money from each of them. Teresa forked over more."

"By then she was close to broke," Pete said. "Whatever she could carry without arousing suspicion was in a tiny suitcase."

"What a horrible man," Sherri said, disgusted.

"The group arrived at the ranch that night," Suzanne said. "There were mattresses in the garage. Food and water too. Everyone had their picture taken, the first step in getting their phony IDs."

"Okay," the Chief said, nodding his head. "Now we see where Mr. Pauley fits in the puzzle."

"The next morning, things got worse," Kathy said. "Much worse. Angelina roamed around. When it was time to go, her mom couldn't find her. One traveler thought she was in the truck. Teresa jumped in and realized her daughter wasn't there. Before she had time to react, Mike Lyons slammed the door shut and drove away."

"With everyone except Angelina," Joe said.

"Right. When they arrived at the depot," Suzanne continued, "Mike Lyons had to deal with a sobbing and hysterical Teresa. He rushed back, searching for the little girl. That's when he passed me on the roadside. He must have spotted our car, but never imagined Angelina had walked from the ranch to the highway."

"And had no clue she was sitting in the car with you!" The coincidence was too much for Sherri.

"Thank the Lord she made it," Maria said.

"What prompted Teresa to get on the bus?" Joe asked.

"Fear," Kathy replied. "If they picked her up as an undocumented immigrant, there was nothing she could do behind bars."

Tom jumped into the conversation. "Mike Lyons assured her that Angelina would catch the next bus with another group. That never happened."

"So she ended up in Phoenix, working for peanuts, trying to pay an exorbitant charge for room and board," Suzanne finished. "That's how the factory trapped her. No phony ID until she pays them off."

"To the last dime," Pete said. "She felt like a slave."

"No kidding," Maria said. "I would too. That is truly heart-breaking."

"Well," the Chief said, "the good news is that we don't have to worry about Mike Lyons any longer."

All eyes focused on him in surprise. "What do you mean?" Suzanne asked.

"We alerted Customs and Border Patrol—remember, I told you I'd have to tell the feds this week—so they've been keeping an eye open for him," the Chief replied. "They picked him up last night, south of Sierra Vista, close to the border. He's under arrest for human smuggling. We won't be seeing him for a long time."

"Darn good thing," Sherri said.

———————

LATER THAT NIGHT, THE TWINS HAD THEIR FIRST OPPORTUNITY TO update their parents on the debacle at Parker Hall's ranch.

"Then the last frame showed up, and there was Hank Pauley," Suzanne concluded. "Staring into the lens. He creeped us right out."

"Uh-oh," his mother interjected, "there goes the equipment you borrowed."

"Don't even think about it," Tom said, groaning. "I'm not looking forward to telling Ray. Here's the shot of Pauley." He held up his cell phone.

The Chief examined the picture. "He doesn't look too happy, does he? Where's the still of the phony IDs?"

Tom rolled over to another frame.

"Yup, not much doubt what that is," the Chief said. "It might be tough to tell the difference between those and the real thing."

"We know they're printing phony driver's licenses for Arizona and California," Tom said. "I wonder if they're doing the whole country?"

"No clue," the Chief said. "I'll alert the feds—but I'm wondering what the next step is for Hank Pauley."

19

UNDER FIRE

Tuesday morning, Suzanne's cell phone buzzed and vibrated, close and insistent, somewhere on her bed. *It's awfully early*, she thought. Exhausted from so many late nights with so little sleep, she rummaged around until she found the darn thing.

"Hello, Neil," she answered without budging from her pillow.

"There's a huge bonfire at Hank Pauley's place," he said. "They've been feeding it since six o'clock. And a large moving truck rolled onto their driveway this morning too."

Suzanne sat up, wide awake now. She put her cell on speaker and stumbled into Tom's bedroom, shaking him.

"We're on our way," Suzanne said. "We should be there in twenty minutes."

Click. He disconnected. Same old Neil. No manners, even when he was being nice.

The twins raced downstairs. Their mother was enjoying breakfast with Teresa and Angelina. They hugged their mom.

"Where's Dad?" Tom asked.

"The department needed him at 5:00 a.m.," Sherri replied.

"Neil Vanderbilt just called," Suzanne said, her words rushing out. "Looks as if Hank Pauley and the boys are up to something.

They're burning stuff out at Parker Hall's ranch. Plus, a large moving van just pulled in."

Teresa couldn't speak a word of English, but she understood excitement. She shot a questioning glance to Sherri.

"¡Adolescentes!" Sherri said, rolling her eyes.

The twins raced upstairs to get dressed. Within five minutes they were on Highway 89, heading north, with Tom at the wheel.

Suzanne messaged Kathy with an update. *Meet u out there,* Kathy replied.

Next, Suzanne called her father. No answer. She messaged him: *Neil Vanderbilt called. Hank Pauley packing up. Bonfire.*

Soon they saw a plume of thick, black smoke soaring into the sky, visible for miles. "Whoa, check it out," Tom exclaimed. "What do you think they're burning?"

"Evidence," Suzanne said.

"Hey, look what's coming."

Suzanne scanned the horizon. "It's the helicopter!"

The twins watched the aircraft dip lower in the skyline until it disappeared below a hill.

Tom turned left and pulled onto Apache Canyon Drive. "Let's drive past the ranch. Can't be any harm doing that."

"Okay."

Parker Hall's place was a circus. Parked on the driveway was Hank Pauley's truck. Two cars sat just outside the garage, their doors all flung open, and the helicopter stood on its landing pad. A moving van was there too, just as Neil had mentioned, its rear door rolled up, the cargo area open and half full. Half a dozen men hurried about, loading heavy equipment and boxes into the van and suitcases and bulging trash bags into the cars.

In the middle of it all, a huge bonfire continued to burn.

As the Chevy broached the entranceway, a guard armed with a shotgun jumped out from behind the industrial garbage bin. *He's waiting for us?* ran through Suzanne's mind. The twins recognized the man from their surveillance photos as one of the computer operators. He flagged them down, walking in front of the car—and pointing his shotgun at the Chevy's windshield.

A startled Tom braked hard and cracked his window, making sure all the Chevy's doors remained locked.

The man leaned toward him. "Looking for your camera equipment?" he asked in a sneering tone.

"How can I help you?" Tom replied, his heart ramped up to high speed.

The man's mouth twisted in an angry snarl. "Out of the car!" he ordered. Attached to his head was a headset microphone.

"No, thanks," Tom said, "We're just passing through." *Someone else was listening,* they realized.

"Get out or I'll blow a hole in your tires!" the man snapped, pointing a shotgun at the Chevy's front wheel, then raising it to the windshield. "Or your heads!"

Hank Pauley appeared from out of nowhere. Suzanne shrunk deeper down into her seat.

"Oh, it's those kids again!" Pauley exclaimed. "So it *was* you all along. I knew you'd be trouble right from the start. *Get out of that car!*"

"No, thanks," Tom responded.

"You don't understand," Hank Pauley raised his voice. "I'm not asking you, I'm ordering you!"

Tom stomped on the gas pedal and the car lunged forward. A huge boom exploded, rocking the vehicle. An intense smell of burning rubber filled the Chevy's cabin. A rear tire had blown into pieces. The car wobbled. Tom braked.

The two men raced to the Chevy. *"Get out, now!"* Pauley roared.

The twins locked eyes. "Okay," Tom said in a grim tone, tracking the muzzle of the shotgun leveled at his face. "There's not much choice."

He unlocked the doors. The twins stepped out, eyes on the shotgun, and walked to the front of the car. They pushed up against one another for safety.

Other workers rushed toward them, accompanied by the

barking German shepherd, set off by the shotgun blast. Pauley waved the men away with one hand.

"Keep loading!" he yelled. "And get that dog out of here!"

He pressed his huge head in Tom's face, breathing hard. His breath was foul—like a moldy ashtray. "Where did the pictures go?"

"Right here," Tom replied, displaying the cell phone in his hand.

"Gimme that!" Pauley ripped it away. He touched the screen and hit Photos. The last pic shown was the scan of the phony drivers' licenses. He glared at the twins. "Yup, we're toast, thanks to you. We spotted your car the night you came out here. It took a lot of searching to find that camera. So this project died, but you're gonna pay a price. You and your twin sister here. A high—"

"Drop that shotgun!" someone roared from behind the car.

Everyone jumped. The twins knew that voice, though they didn't dare turn around to see their rescuer: none other than Neil Vander-bilt. He circled the Chevy, stopping just a few feet short of Hank Pauley and the computer operator. His shotgun, held tight against his shoulder in shooting position, threatened both men at point-blank range.

"Drop it," he said once more. It was a voice you didn't dare argue with. "And—get—those—hands—*up!*"

The operator meekly dropped his weapon onto the gravel road-way. Both men raised their hands.

"Neil!" Suzanne blurted out in relief. And now, standing beside the twins, a grinning Pete and Kathy, who had been following behind. "Boy, are we glad to see you." She wrapped her two best friends in an enormous hug at the same time.

Tom snatched the shotgun off the gravel road.

"Aim it at chest level, Tom," Neil ordered. "Hold steady. But keep your finger off the trigger."

Tom followed instructions to the letter. "He has my phone."

"Give it back!" Neil ordered.

Pauley tossed Tom's phone to the ground.

"Now, don't move, you two!" Neil ordered. Pauley and his henchman froze in place.

Sirens blared. Everyone turned to see three Yavapai County Sheriff's vehicles racing toward them, sending up a cloud of dust into the morning air. Neil and Tom took their eyes off their captives for only an instant, but it was enough: Pauley and the technician bolted, leaping over the fence.

"Let'em go," Neil said. "They won't get far."

The police vehicles ground to a halt behind the Chevy and its blown-out tire. County Sheriff Steve McClennan and two of his deputies sprinted out of their cars.

The sheriff spotted the four friends—he had known them since childhood. But he stared with suspicion at the unknown man holding a shotgun.

"Sir, you need to drop that weapon onto the road."

Neil set it down, gently. Tom had already lowered the technician's gun to the ground, relieved not to have to keep pretending he had the slightest idea how to use it.

"He's okay, Sheriff," Tom assured the sheriff. "He saved us from the two guys who just ran away."

"Along with the Brunellis," Suzanne said with a huge smile.

"We didn't do a thing!" their friends protested in unison.

Without warning, the helicopter fired up and, moments later, lifted skyward. As it passed overhead, Pauley's huge head emerged, scowling out from the cockpit passenger window.

"Thank goodness he's gone," Suzanne said.

Kathy nodded. "You're not kidding. That man's a menace to society."

"Which means we have to catch him!" said the sheriff, jumping with his deputies back into their cars and speeding through the ranch's gate.

Minutes later, the Chief arrived, smiling and ecstatic to learn that his band of homegrown mystery searchers had cracked the case wide open—with a little help from their newfound friend. Suzanne turned to introduce Neil and the Chief to each other—but Neil had disappeared. Baffled, she tried to explain how he had saved the twins from Pauley's clutches.

"He's cool," explained Pete, the only one of the four who had not met Neil previously. "We turned onto Apache Canyon Drive and found him walking toward Vanderbilt's ranch."

"Armed with his shotgun," Kathy added.

Pete described how the bonfire had gotten Neil's attention early in the morning. The rancher had figured Hank Pauley must be up to no good. Later, he had driven across 89, parked his car, and walked the rest of the way to attract less attention.

"We said we were worried about Suzanne and Tom," Kathy added, glancing toward the twins, "because you had stopped messaging. Neil told us to park our car and follow him."

Soon a fleet of vehicles were descending on the scene as the story leaked out over police radios. A photographer from *The Daily Pilot* arrived, with the winsome Heidi Hoover trailing behind him. The local television channel deployed their huge broadcast van, streaming live footage on TV and over the internet. Worried neighbors parked out front. The four friends handled dozens of questions.

Sheriff McClennan was busy processing an enormous crime scene. "That guy with the shotgun is a hero," he said to everyone within earshot. "Say, where is he, anyway?"

The words of Officer Kurt Jenkins, spoken a couple weeks earlier, echoed in Suzanne's mind: *People love hero stories.*

"Maybe not everyone wants to be a hero," she said.

118

20

A HERO'S REWARD

Tom sat outside on the Jacksons' lawn, waiting for Wednesday's morning newspaper. It soon landed on the driveway with a soft thud.

He rushed out and flipped the paper over in his hands. The Jackson twins and their two friends had made the front page.

"Suzie, get down here!" he shouted. "You gotta see this!"

"Teens crack cases wide open" read the headline. Underneath was a secondary caption, "Major counterfeiters arrested." Toward the bottom of the page appeared another story, "Mother and child reunited."

The lead article detailed the counterfeiting at the ranch and the arrests at Scottsdale Municipal Airport. "After discovering hundreds of counterfeit driver's licenses, police arrested the pilot of the helicopter and one passenger. Other warrants are pending. A police spokeswoman said the phony-ID operation was the largest of its type in recent Arizona history. The helicopter's cargo included fake licenses from Arizona, Texas, California, Michigan, and New York. The value of the haul exceeded an estimated one million dollars."

A shot of the four accompanied the article. They smiled toward the camera, arms linked around each other's shoulders.

"That's an awful picture of me," Suzanne complained with a scowl.

"It looks just like you," her brother teased.

"Who asked you, hotshot?"

Another image captured Parker Hall's ranch, with county police cars and officers swarming the driveway. A third shot focused on Neil Vanderbilt, standing on the porch between his two dogs.

"Look," said Tom, pointing at the picture. He couldn't help grinning. "Neil's still holding his shotgun."

"I'm sure he wasn't too happy to see those reporters," Suzanne said, recalling the girls' first trip to Apache Canyon Drive.

Teresa was at the breakfast table, visiting with Sherri. Angelina sat down in Suzanne's lap, eating cereal.

The Brunellis soon called and there was no holding back Kathy's excitement. "Did your paper arrive? What a great picture of Neil. Those reporters are lucky they didn't catch a load of buckshot."

Maria's laugh pealed in the background.

A DAY LATER, AS TOM DROVE ONTO NEIL'S RANCH, A FAMILIAR SIGHT loomed before them. The bedraggled man, relaxing on his front porch, smoking a cigar, watched them with a wary expression. His dogs lay beside him.

The Chevy pulled up and ground to a halt. As the twins stepped out of the car, the dogs rushed out to greet them. Neil whistled, calling them back beside him.

"Whadaya want?" he growled.

"We came out to thank you," Tom said.

"You're welcome." He had a surly edge to his voice. "Thanks for visiting and goodbye."

"Neil," Suzanne said, "we need to talk. It's important." She felt apprehensive herself.

"So talk," he said, grunting. The twins found seats on the weather-beaten porch. But Neil did most of the talking. He shared his story, bit by bit—a confession, really—that explained everything about the Unknown Caller.

LATER THAT EVENING, THE TWINS DESCRIBED THEIR VISIT FOR THE Brunelli siblings, Chief Jackson, and Sherri.

"Poor guy," Kathy said with a sorrowful look. "Just one mistake."

"In my experience, one mistake is all it takes," the Chief said.

"Can you help him?" Sherri asked her husband.

"That depends on the authorities in Coweta County, Georgia," he replied. "I'm guessing they might be open to dropping the charges. The man broke out of jail when he was sixteen. It was half a century ago, and the original charge—a burglary committed by an underage child—landed him in there. Plus," he added, "Mr. Vanderbilt is a hero, a good citizen." The Chief paused, looking very serious, as his eyes passed over the four mystery searchers. "He may even have saved your lives."

"His real name is Tom Burlingham," Tom said.

"Ah, yes. You mentioned that he had changed his identity," the Chief said. He jotted down the name. "Another bad choice."

"But this time he made the *right* choice," Suzanne said. "Even though it was a difficult one. One phone call could expose him, and he always knew it."

"And that's exactly what happened," Pete said.

"He must have been lonely," Kathy said. "He hid for many years."

"Maybe he won't have to be so lonely anymore," Sherri said.

IT TURNED OUT THAT RAYDON PAPER COMPANY ITSELF HAD NOTHING to do with the counterfeiting operation. The perpetrators were a rogue unit within the company. They had grabbed an opportunity to make millions—and failed. One morning the president of Raydon called, offering to replace the camera equipment destroyed by his ex-employees. The four friends were ecstatic.

So was Ray. "New stuff, great!" he exclaimed when Tom delivered the news.

Parker Hall was innocent. The counterfeiters had convinced him they were working for the U.S. government on a top-secret mission.

"Gosh, I'm sorry," Mr. Hall said, when the four friends met at Hall's Hardware at his invitation. "Hank Pauley flashed a phony badge and swore me to secrecy. When you came by," he said, addressing the twins, "I had to cover up for him. I was uncomfortable and let him know."

"No problem, Mr. Hall," Tom said. "It all worked out fine."

After considering her options, Teresa announced her decision to return home. The four friends began a crowdfunding drive for mother and daughter. Because her story had gone national, money flowed in—enough to pay for airfare *and to* fund a fresh start for the little family back home in Mexico.

A few days later the Jackson and Brunelli families drove to Prescott Municipal Airport. "'Thank you so much,'" Suzanne translated for Teresa as the little girl hugged each of her new friends. "'None of this would be possible without you.'" Angelina's eyes were bigger than saucers. She cried as she wrapped her arms around Suzanne.

"Tú y tu mamá nos pueden visitar en cualquier momento," Suzanne said, comforting the little girl. She looked up at Teresa, her friends, her brother, her parents, all beaming. "I said they can visit us anytime."

ONE DAY, HALF WAY THROUGH THE SUMMER, THE CHIEF RECEIVED A call from the sheriff of Coweta County, Georgia. The state's attorney general had agreed to drop all charges against Thomas Burlingham.

Neil still refused to answer his cell phone, so Suzanne texted him: *Great news. We're coming out to see you—now!*

The four friends, Chief Jackson, and Sheriff Steve McClennan all descended on the Vanderbilt ranch. The enthusiastic committee shocked Neil—and his dogs.

Everyone gathered around to deliver the big news. "You are a free man," Suzanne said, beaming. "Coweta County has dropped the charges against you."

As gruff as they come, Neil still couldn't hide his happiness. The shadow on his life had lifted.

"Thank you," he said in a subdued voice. Kathy swore she saw a shimmer of tears in the corners of his eyes.

"It's not too often," Sheriff McClennan said, "that I shake hands with a genuine hero."

"We all owe you a debt of gratitude," the Chief said.

"Well, what should we call you now?" Kathy asked him. "Tom or Neil?"

"I need to think on that. I've been Neil Vanderbilt for a long time."

Soon enough, the celebration ended. Neil stood in his driveway and waved goodbye. He shook hands with the boys but couldn't escape hugs from the girls.

"That guy is stiff as a board," Kathy said on the way home.

ANOTHER FEW DAYS PASSED BEFORE THE CHIEF DELIVERED astonishing news.

"Hank Pauley has been talking to the FBI. He's working out a deal to reduce his jail time. Remember those two guys who gave Mike Lyons a hard time?"

"Sure," Tom said. "The ones who walked out to 89 with him."

"Correct. Turns out those two had dozens of folks like Mike Lyons working for them, all over the country. They partnered with

Hank Pauley to get phony IDs for the migrant workers they smuggled in. The two cases have now become one."

"So there *was* a direct connection," Suzanne said.

"I knew it," Pete said.

"That's funny. You never mentioned it before," his sister bugged.

"Another thing," the Chief continued, looking at his twins. "We learned why Pauley stopped behind you on 89."

"And freaked me right out with his imaginary gun," Suzanne said. The twins sat bold upright, hanging onto their father's every word. "Why?"

"Tom parked at the only place on 89 that offers a view of the ranch. Straight to the barn's front door, in fact. It opened just as Pauley drove by. He wanted to make sure you weren't spying on them. And he didn't want you coming back—ever."

Suzanne stifled a grin. "No way! That was a huge mistake on his part. If he hadn't stopped, we'd never have tied him to Parker Hall's ranch."

Tom nodded. "In which case his counterfeiting operation would still be rolling along."

Kathy agreed. "Nothing more than bad luck—for him."

"We sure caught some lucky breaks," Pete declared.

"That's what mystery searchers do," the Chief said. "They work hard, searching for a lucky break or two. And knowing how to take advantage of those breaks makes all the difference. Your success proves it."

Suzanne's cell phone rang. She glanced at the screen. Dr. William Wasson. "Never heard of him," she said, thinking out loud.

"Hello?" She listened for a minute, then covered up the cell phone's microphone. Her eyes danced.

"Oh my gosh, you won't believe it. This man's asking for our help. We've got another mystery to solve!"

EXCERPT FROM BOOK 2

THE GHOST IN THE COUNTY COURTHOUSE

Chapter 1
All for Nothing

"But that's impossible, sir!" Tom blurted.

Sixteen-year-old twins Tom and Suzanne Jackson and their best friends, Pete and Kathy Brunelli, glanced at one another, baffled. They were sitting across a desk from Dr. William Wasson, the dean of Aztec College and the curator of the Yavapai Courthouse Museum. The dean had called them to an emergency Friday-morning meeting at the museum one hour before its opening to the public.

It was a fine day in early July. The Jacksons and Brunellis were fresh off their adventures on Apache Canyon Drive, a rural area just north of their mountain city home of Prescott, Arizona—"Everybody's hometown." Their success in foiling a cruel migrant-laborer smuggling and counterfeiting ring—and restoring a lost little girl from Mexico to her mother—was not only front-page news in *The*

Daily Pilot, Prescott's hometown newspaper. The story had gone national. "Four young mystery searchers had solved the cases," it read. Local ones too.

The drama captured Dean Wasson from word one: "Mystery searchers." He repeated it later to his staff, "Just what we need."

The dean was a tall man in his sixties, distinguished-looking, with short gray hair and steel-rimmed glasses; he wore a white shirt and tie. Worry had etched his face. "Yes, you're right: it is impossible—or ought to be. Yet *someone* or *something* emerges at will and we're powerless to stop it." He shrugged his shoulders. "It's grotesque for sure. The museum staff calls it a ghost but we don't really believe that, of course. Then again, tell me what else walks through walls and bypasses the security system as if it doesn't exist!"

Kathy, official notetaker and the youngest member of the team, scribbled away at high speed, her eyes darting around the room.

"Is there a pattern to the ghost's appearances?" Pete asked. He was the impetuous one who always went straight to the point. "Like a particular day of the week?"

"Yes, and it's a strange one," the dean replied, peering at them over his glasses. "The ghost arrives *to the minute* —at two-oh-four a.m.—each time, but the nights are random. We haven't a clue if he'll show up tonight, sometime next week, or ever again, for that matter."

He paused, deep in thought. Seconds from a circular wall clock pierced the silence with a deadened sound.

"Hopefully, he—or she, or it—won't ever return, but we have our doubts. Our budget is tight—we're still in a fund-raising mode for all the renovations. No way can we afford to pay for a security guard here overnight, every night."

"Has anyone actually *seen* this ghost?" Suzanne asked, trying to wrap her mind around it.

"Oh, for certain!" Dean Wasson exclaimed. "The first time the mysterious thing appeared, it triggered the motion detectors. Strange, because there was no sign of a break-in. How would our system detect an immaterial entity? I've always wondered what the —well, whatever it is—was trying to tell us, because the alarm never activated again. We can't figure out why."

"When did this occur?" Tom asked. He was the quiet, thoughtful one. Every word counted.

"It was May twenty-second," the dean replied. "Roger Holloway, our custodian, received an emergency call from the security company. It was after two a.m. That call *should* have gone to our director, Gloria Waldner, but she was out on vacation. Roger lives just a few blocks away. He rushed over, arriving ahead of the police, and looked through the windows. A ghostly figure was moving through the displays. Shimmering white from head to toe. Scared poor Roger witless."

"Oh, wow, what happened next?" Kathy paused in her note taking. She shuddered. Could there be a ghost, after all? *Was it even possible?*

"The police arrived, but it was too late. The ghost was long gone." Dean Wasson lowered his voice. "At first, they didn't believe him, but I sure did. Roger doesn't make things up."

Kathy shook her head and sat up straighter. She continued to write, wide-eyed and alert.

"It didn't trigger the alarm after that first visit?" Pete asked.

"Never," the dean replied. "And since then the problem has only gotten worse. Much worse. Two priceless Hohokam relics—or artifacts, as we sometimes call them in archeology—disappeared one night just over a week later, on June third. They are—they were— the pride of our collection. That event threw us into a full-blown crisis."

"So at that point, the 'ghost' had visited twice and stolen two relics, both during its second appearance—but set off the alarm only the first time?" Tom asked.

"Correct."

"Then I'd say that whoever the thief is, he *wanted* the police—or someone on your staff—to see him during the first incursion. If the thief can disable or evade your security system, then he must have *wanted* you to see him in his ghost disguise."

"Maybe to distract you, even to make you panic," Pete said.

"Right," Suzanne added. Her confident style always impressed people. "He wasn't worried about getting caught, either."

"Quite so," Dean Wasson said, most impressed with their sober reasoning. "All of that sounds reasonable, and the detective assigned to the case said so too. But that still doesn't answer the burning question." He stood up and stared out the window toward Whiskey Row—Prescott's historic downtown street—with unseeing eyes.

"What's that, sir?" Kathy asked.

"How does it enter the museum?" the dean replied. A forefinger stabbed the air for emphasis. "How and *where*? Once lockdown occurs, no one gets in—or out. It's impossible."

"Are there any clues at all?" Suzanne asked.

"None." Dean Wasson turned back toward his visitors. "We've had multiple meetings with Prescott City Police officials in this office. They're as mystified as I am." The dean glanced over at the twins. "Your father is the chief of police."

"Yes, sir," Tom said. "He asked us to help in any way possible."

"We'll do everything we can," Suzanne said, trying to comfort the poor man. He appeared to be suffering from intense anxiety.

The dean smiled for the first time since his guests had arrived. "Please extend my thanks to your father. I know the department has worked hard on the case. They had a plain-clothes officer keep the place under covert surveillance every night for a week." He peered over his glasses. "Any idea what happened?"

"The Chief briefed us, sir," Suzanne replied. "The ghost failed to appear."

"Yes, correct again." The dean sat down, his chest visibly heaving. "Most disheartening—and a little suspicious. The detective in charge questioned us about the possibility of an inside job, of course. After all, my staff were the only ones who knew about the policeman. Who told the ghost?" He sighed again, louder this time, and sadder too.

"It's a bitter pill when one considers how we began," Dean Wasson continued. "The museum moved here—to the ground floor of the Yavapai County Courthouse—last fall. This majestic building is Prescott's finest, the jewel of the city, and a center of our cultural life. The cornerstone dates to 1916, well over a century ago. We're very proud of its history, but you know all that." The dean looked at the four best friends for confirmation. All born and raised in Prescott, they nodded.

"We played hide-and-seek on the courthouse steps when we were little," Kathy recalled, bringing a smile to everyone's faces. Those steps were part of Prescott's lore. Summer nights brought popular music festivals to Courthouse Plaza. Among the hundreds of people who crowded into the park, dozens found seating on the spacious stepped entrance to the famous old courthouse.

Dean Wasson stood up once more and paced his office floor. His gestures reflected the strained tone of his voice. "The location is perfect, much better than our previous quarters on campus. The museum has always been part of Aztec College, but we function quite independently. We have room to grow now. The structure— constructed from handsome granite quarried right here in Prescott —is a well-built architectural wonder. The design is even inspirational. Look at these windows." He pointed to one. "Plenty of natural light, which we filter to preserve our fragile textiles and so on. We raised the funds to install high-security windows and doors. And the museum boasts a fine alarm system." He exhaled audibly once more. "All for nothing. It has failed to protect our most valuable relics."

The dean paused, observing people as they strolled across the courthouse grounds. He cranked the window open. Birds sang from the dozens of American elm trees that ringed the building. Sounds of children laughing and playing in the surrounding four-acre park filtered into the office. The smell of fresh-cut grass wafted up around them. A mosquito settled on Tom's arm. He smacked it.

Once again, the dean turned toward them. He shook his head in disgust. "As I said, a month ago a major theft occurred. That was a terrible day. Everything seemed fine when we arrived at the museum that morning. But then—"

There was a sudden knock at the door.

We hope you enjoyed this sneak peak at
The Ghost in the County Courthouse
Pick up your copy at your favorite retailer today!

ABOUT THE AUTHOR

Barry Forbes, an award-winning industrial film and video writer and producer, engages his technology background and love of mystery to enthrall, entertain and mystify middle-grade tweens and teens from eleven to fifteen years of age.

Read more at www.MysterySearchers.com

Made in the USA
San Bernardino, CA
11 May 2020

71168372R00078